THE MADNESS OF AVLON KLYNN

-------- BOOK ONE --------

CREATED BY
RICHARD TODD

𝓔

Eloquent Books
New York, New York

Richard Todd

Eloquent Books
An imprint of Writers Literary & Publishing Services, Inc.
845 Third Avenue, 6th Floor – 6016
New York, NY 10022
www.eloquentbooks.com

ISBN: 978-1-934925-45-4 / ISBN/SKU: 1-934925-45-4

Printed in the United States of America

Book Design: Mark Bredt
Cover Illustration © Algol / DreamsTime.com

I dedicate this to my dad
who lives on in my heart…

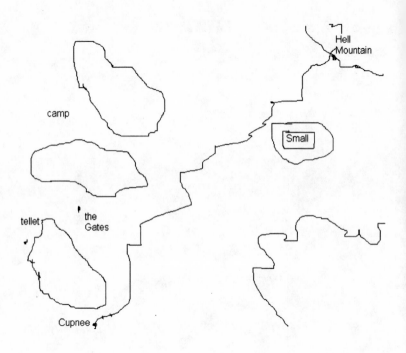

Hell
Mountain

camp

Small

tellet

the
Gates

Cupnee

CHAPTER 1

As wind blew around the softness of the grass, but a gentle whisper carried over the plains and into the evil land of Breaker where evil things lived and breathed. However, on this night a small party of elves sat around their campfire not giving a care about the world about them, they knew evil was in the field with them nevertheless, they ignored it for now. If need be they would be alerted to fight off the vampires or anything else that tried to attack them.

A small fire was on; over it was a pot of stew from the night before. Left over's it had to be eaten .One of the elves looked over his shoulder as his hair got in his way as he looked at the lone sentry he brushed aside his shoulder length hair that blew in the wind as he gathered the last of the food onto the plate.

"Bremin, I have some food here," Kinler said as he passed the plate of food to his friend, Bremin stood up from the ground since he was sitting and took a few steps toward his friend that had long brown hair that covered his ears. His angular features were soft to look at, even his eyes.

Accepting the offered meat and vegetables Bremin smiled, grateful for the food, since he was hungry from the long trek from the day before.

"Thank you." Bremin said then added, after he took a bit of his meal. "We shouldn't be here," he warned the rest of his friends. His closely chopped silver hair didn't bother him as he studied his surroundings; he bit into the meat for the first time he smiled tasting the juice remembering when his own mother had made this dish four years ago before he left to rejoin this particular hunting group. It was his second term with the hunting party but it was nearing its end, he didn't want to split up again.

"Don't worry. We'll be fine." Sonel said as his golden yellow hair blew around him as he tried not to scratch a rash that he got earlier from a poison flower that he had fallen on the day before, but he scratched it any way to relieve himself, but it only made it worse.

"We should be in that wood over there and up a tree," Bremin said. He was trying to stay calm, but it was hard for him. He took another bite of his food and he enjoyed it. Still he would not let it go, his friends were risking their lives, for what, Bremin thought. Do they know something that I don't?

The others heard him, as did the five vampires that laid in waiting in the stillness of the night. Bremin watched the four drift off into slumber a few minutes later. He knew he was right, but what puzzled him was why his friends would want trouble at the early hours of the morning. Holding his bow ready for any kind of attack, he heard a branch break. It made him jump a little. He looked to his left, then to his right, gazing into the dark forest. Something moved near the forest. Adjusting his eyesight to see what it was, Bremin smiled; it was only a fox exploring the area for food.

I must be getting jumpy, Bremin thought, as he sat down on a log a few feet away.

"Rest," the wind said, and the lone elf looked around trying to see who had said the single word, he fought off the impulse to go to sleep but he spotted nothing except a falling leaf that the wind had blow up from the ground. He could see the field he was in, but not into the shadowed areas where the vampires had stayed hidden from sight. The mountains could be seen beyond the forest, and yet Bremin felt lightheaded.

No need to worry, he thought and lay down right beside the log that shielded him from sight from the clearing. A second later, he was fast asleep. He rolled over in his sleep and went into a small ditch that would shield him from sight even from his friends.

Slowly the five normal faced vampires came into the camp, each making their way to their prey. None of them made a sound. The campfire kept on burning, as the vampires were hoping not to wake the elves at all. All of them knew where their target was each, but the fifth looked around not sure where his victim had gone.

"Where the hell is he?" he asked his friends hopping to get a good answer as he looked around not seeing his intended victim.

"Don't know. He must have escaped," said one of the vampires as he gazed down at his victim, which was on the right side of his friend. He then sank his teeth into the elf's neck a second later. Getting back up to his feet the vampire glanced around him surveying the land he wiped the blood away with the back side of his hand. The rest of his friends drained the blood from the last of the elves, the vampires smiled at each other once they were satisfied but their friend needed to feed.

"I know where some food is," a closely cut black haired vampire said, as he showed his fangs. His features were dark, since it was night. You couldn't tell what his features were, but noticed that the sun was coming up slowly.

"To the forest," one of the vampires urged his friends and ran toward the dark forest.

As the sun crested the horizon, a lone hooded man studied the scene before him. It didn't spook him; he felt sorry for the elves that lay there. He felt he knew what could have prevented it from happening if he got there earlier. Bending over one of the elves, the druid studied the markings on the male's neck, it was only the brisk of dawn before it was light; he detected movement out of the corner of his eye.

"You killed them!" Bremin accused the druid as he raised his sword, but he didn't know who it was that stood before him, he held his sword at the ready, to avenge his kindred at any cost.

"Don't," the druid warned. "Your kin were killed by vampires."

Bremin raised his sword even more, not believing a word.

"You lie," he gasped, but the druid turned one of the heads to the side, the elf looked at the marks on the neck of one of his friends. The sword dropped from his hands, it hit the ground as he fell to the ground, saddened by his loss. Bremin had traveled the lands with them for four full years, fighting off their enemies and hiding from the evil master that plagued the land with his vast army of gnomes, trolls, vampires, and God knows what. However, this latest act had forced his hand; Bremin knew he had to unite the others to destroy the evil master and his legion once and for all.

Looking at the hooded man that stood before him for

the first time, he realized he could not see the man's eyes. "Who are you? What are you?" Bremin questioned sharply hoping who ever stood before him would answer.

The druid took the hood off as a reply as his shoulder length white hair blew in the breeze as did the foot long beard. He stood there, confident of his abilities as he watched the elf with interest.

Bremin staggered back a step surprised to see the famous druid Randle. He knew who the man was since the druid had helped the elves long ago. Bremin remembered those days when he was only a child, so full of life and willing to go on adventures that were not for the faint of heart. Randle had helped them destroy the Noarta sword that housed the spirit of an evil king that was called Firold, which wanted to destroy the elves for good, which was only five years ago.

"Come, we can do nothing for them," said Randle as he reached out to touch the other's hand. The elf gazed at the hand not willing to grab onto it but he knew that it was out of friend ship .Bremin grabbed it and forced a smile, Bremin could tell by the handshake that Arcan was stronger than he had thought.

"We have much to do," Randle announced, and the elf knew what the druid was talking about or thought he did. They left the four dead bodies to burn in the morning light. Tears came to Bremin's eyes saddened by his loss, but Randle urged him away from the scene. Not willing to take on any more problems.

As they traveled over the field, neither of them spoke a word. Each and every flower filled their sight, which pleased the two. Randle just thought about the future while Bremin remembered his old friends. He was heart broken since this was the first time he had ever lost a friend, or friends, for this matter. On they traveled, passing a stream of water as a few birds flew overhead.

Strolling toward the small village, Arcan noticed the size of it. It only had ten houses all looked as if they were repaired from a recent storm. Bremin smiled at the sight of the flowers, just off the edge of the town. Onward they strolled as; both of them gazed at the beauty that lay before them. A single stall filled with all sorts of things. It had water bottles and baked goods. Off to its side, a merchant was selling rugs. Each was being shown on display, as two females were working hard to make a living.

There was a single inn that stood off to their left; its sign read Falling Star. Nothing was out of place. A doctor's cabin was next door to the inn. Its sign read Sam's Attention.

Randle glanced at his newfound friend as he indicated that he was going over to one of the stalls. In the centre of the village, a single tree stood in full bloom. Its leaves were starting to fall, since it was the season for it. It was surrounded by grass that a few children ran on. Some played warrior or pretended to have grand adventures of a sort. A smiled formed on Bremin's face, seeing how happy everyone was, it pleased him.

Bremin looked about him as he studied the village; he knew that this village was one of the protected. This village was known as the Gates, and he now knew why it was called this. It was peaceful.

"Why are we here?" Bremin asked trying to find out what the druid was about to do.

The druid glanced at him briefly.

"We need food and supplies. We might as well get something to eat while we're here," Randle said as his stomach which growled with hunger.

Bremin nodded at the suggestion since he hadn't eaten anything since he had woke up. It had grieved him to see his friends lying dead. Now nothing mattered to him all he wanted now was to avenge his fallen comrades.

"Did you hear what I said?" Randle asked, but Bremin shook his head, trying to clear his head of the cobwebs that hung in it.

"I'm sorry, Randle." Bremin glanced at the ground." I just keep on thinking about my friends"

"I know how you feel; I lost friends over the years as well." Randle decided to change the subject altogether. "Since we're going to Tellet, we will be needing supplies."

"Tellet?" the elf repeated back, slightly surprised by the name of the elven city, not knowing what the druid was up to. "Why are we going to Tellet? What are we supposed to do there?" Bremin wondered aloud, not sure what Randle Arcan Lee had planned.

"You will find out in due time," Randle replied, trying not to smile since it would only be rude to do so.

The ground rushed past the running halfling's feet as they kicked up a few leaves. He ran for his life. Tree branches swiped at him every which way. Terror filled the little man to the core, but he knew he had to get away from his pursuers.

"Stop running," a jumper yelled at the small creature. "I won't hurt you," it lied.

A half gnome/half bird known as a jumper landed just off to the halfling's right, just inches away, causing him to stumble. He kept on going. Not taking care where he went, he knew that he had to see the famous druid. He noticed a break within the trees and the outline of the small village in the far distance.

"'Bout time," he thought aloud. "Must get to The Gates," he urged himself.

He then felt his legs getting heavy from all the running. He stumbled, pulled himself up as much as he could.

A jumper landed in front of him. He jumped to his right just in time as he brushed up against a tree, which was near to the open field. The last of the trees tore at his shirt as he exited the forest, but he forced himself to keep running. The halfling was beyond tired, as he ran, he couldn't stop not now at least.

"You can't escape us," a single jumper snarled at him as it slashed at him, only missing the halfling by an inch.

By now, the people of the village were noticing the pursuit and started to murmur amongst themselves as they watched from a good distance. The halfling ran as fast as he could, the three pursuers tried to catch up, but the halfling seemed to dodge out of their range.

The halfling ran into the village and ran straight toward a woman.

As Randle picked up two water bottles for his journey ahead, he heard two people collide into each other. He looked up to see what had happened. He also noticed two beings running toward the village. One of them was a jumper, the other looked like a troll and a gnome meshed together, known as a watch.

"YOU CANNOT ENTER," he yelled at them as he raised his hands a thin red line shot forward enforcing the shield even more. Both creatures hit an invisible wall, but a third stopped short as it spotted the magic shield just in time. The two rebounded like rubber balls. The jumper landed on its feet, while the other lay still on the grass, its head lolling unattached since the neck had snapped from the impact. The jumper picked up the dead body of the watch.

"We're not done here," the third, an Orc, cried out as it picked up his fallen comrade and strolled away from the village with its head held high, confident that they would be able to attack the village when the druid was gone.

Walking over to the two who had collided, Randle offered the woman his hand, getting her back to her feet. She grabbed the halfling by the neck since she was mad.

"You dirty little rodent," she spat trying to strangle the halfling with her hands.

"I'm sorry," he replied.

"Put him down," Randle told the woman as he looked at her. A thin smiled was on his face enjoying the moment.

"No, this rodent smashed into me. I rather wring its neck," she replied not willing to let the halfling go from her grip.

"I don't think that would be wise," Randle cautioned trying not to interfere with the lay lady since she wouldn't willing to let go of the halfling then thought better of it as she let go a second later. Back on his feet, the halfling smiled up at the seven-foot man who had aided him.

"I'm here to see Randle Arcan Lee," it said pleased to be free from the woman's grip.

"Arcan," the druid looked deliberately mystified. "I know of him," said Randle, being careful not to reveal his identity to the halfling just yet, but he was surprised because they usually weren't meant to travel outside their own villages since they would sell their family to traders or trick others into doing something that they shouldn't be doing.

"Can you take me to him?" Zek wondered. The druid

nodded in agreement. Zek studied the features of the man; his chin was rounded and smoothed as was the nose, and they held wisdom. The stance of the druid was very confident, as if nothing evil could deter him from his goal.

"I can, but I need to know why you seek him." Randle tried to sound as if he didn't care in the least.

"My village was attacked by Avlon's army. I hid but they found me and attacked me, so I ran here for two full days." Zek said truthfully. His features were sloppy as if someone had hit them with a pole. The nose looked broken, yet the eyes were as hard as ice as if it had seen hard times. Hearing the news, all the nearby villagers just stared at the little man, not sure if they should believe him at all.

"He's making it up," a villager said.

"I bet he's a spy," another piped up.

The druid could see the situation was getting out of hand.

"Do you take us for fools, little man?" Randle said calmly trying to have an open mind why the halfling had sought him out.

"No," the halfling said, looking depressed by the villager's reaction. "They killed my family," he sobbed, as tears ran down his cheeks. Pain laced through its body, but Zek ignored it for now, it was hurting and no one believed his story. The druid noticed a red mark on the halfling's shoulder.

"What's this?" he exclaimed, pulling the remains of the shirt off the halfling seeing the claw marks on the back. "Dear God, the halfling is telling the truth," which stunned the crowd of people. Randle studied the marks to see exactly what had broken the skin. "Get a doctor," the druid urged. "These claw marks were from…" and his face went white. "What's your name, little one?"

"Zek," he replied, trying not to cry out in pain.

"Zek, you'll be all right," Randle said. "Just do what the doctor here tells you."

"What do you think, Doctor?" he asked as the doctor rushed over from the small crowd of people. He only stood at a normal size which was only five nine. He looked as if nothing had troubled him, but was willing to help the halfling. Sam was a good man; he would do anything to help a fellow man or halfling in need. Leaning down he studied the halfling's shoulder and its back, he could see that the halfling had cuts over its back and a few whip marks.

"Not good," Sam replied concerned for the halfling.

"Hilda, take him to the medic tent," the doctor commanded, the woman led Zek away.

"What do you think attacked him?" the druid asked his old friend.

"Gnomes, or it might have been a jumper," the doctor mused, "but I hesitate to take a guess. It's some type of gnome attack." He ran his hand over the long dark hair that went to his shoulders. He then added, "This halfling has cuts all over his back as well, even whip marks."

The doctor turned away only to hear his name once more from his druid friend.

"Thanks, Sam," Randle said, since he was concerned for the halfling, which was a surprise to him as he watched his friend return to his tent.

"Why would a gnome want to capture a halfling?" Bremin asked, and then thought of the watch. Usually a party of gnomes would have a runner with them, not a watch. It puzzled both of them.

"Zek is coming with us, isn't he?" Bremin said, displeased with the idea but Randle looked at him sternly.

The druid nodded his head slightly.

"Thought so. I just don't trust him," he warned.

"Neither do I. It's just something doesn't add up. That's why he has to come with us," Randle said with determination. "I just need to find out his angle in all of this."

Coming home after a week's journey, Tern and his two, elven friends studied the surrounding area but could not see any of their sentries, which puzzled them at first. Tern had the impression that something was wrong. Looking about them carefully, Tern noticed that several of the trees were marked with claws, which warned him and his two friends. Getting further into their home village of Canor, the three suddenly realized that the shadows moved.

"Guys, we'd better leave," T'lof said, noticing that the village was empty. There were no bodies to be found on the ground. The other two glanced at each other nervously; all three bolted for the field of Premlin. As they ran, the grass whipped at their shoes.

Tern risked looking back over his shoulder.

"Watchers," he gasped. "Lentoplus, shoot them now," he commanded.

Lentoplus stopped running. So did T'lof. They drew back on their bows and shot at the oncoming creatures, but the creatures didn't stagger nor stop. A gnome appeared out of the bush only to be hit in the eye with an arrow. One of the jumpers screeched madly and jumped into the air. Firing off an arrow, T'lof realized one of the jumpers was gone. It was his last thought as the jumper crashed onto him.

Lentoplus went wide-eyed in fear at the scene. Not wishing to suffer the same fate as his brother, he called out his friend's name.

"Tern!" and spotted the forest where his friend had gone. Rushing as fast as he could go, he finally saw his old friend.

"Where's your brother?" Tern asked trying to see where he was, as Lentoplus shot him an angry look.

"Dead," he told his silver-haired friend who had it down to his shoulder.

"I'm so sorry," Tern said. "I'll kill the one that killed him."

"No, he was my brother," Lentoplus said brokenly, so sure that he should be the one to avenge his brothers death.

"No time to argue. Run, Lentoplus," Tern said as he watched his dear friend run as fast as he could.

Turning to see his enemy, he looked up fast. "Snit," he managed to say and dived behind a tree, hoping that the watcher didn't see him. The on rushing enemy gained ground, unaware of the hidden elf, since he had climbed a nearby tree to safety.

Reaching the other side of the forest, Lentoplus spotted the village known as The Gates.

"Looks like a trail," Lentoplus said to himself panting with exertion. He noticed that branches were broken as he ran; he did a quick study of them. Lentoplus knew it was made by a halfling, he gazed ahead of him.

Looking out at the fields of Premlin, Bremin smiled at the sight of the flowers and the tress of the small wood he turned his gaze to another part of the field and noticed a lone elf running toward them. "Randle," Bremin yelled and the druid came out of a tent with something in his mouth.

"You don't have to yell, you know." Randle said as he spotted the enemy chasing the lone elf. He shook his head, not believing his luck for his day. Randle had had enough of Avlon's troops for the day, but luck was not with them. Every day of the year, the great army that Avlon had always meant trouble, no matter where you were.

"That's Lentoplus, a friend of mine," Bremin informed the druid and the others. The druid lowered his hand and swallowed the last of the meat,   Lent jumped into the village just in time, before the druid raised his hand again, putting the invisible shield back up. He twisted back just in time to see the watchers bounce back off the shield, killing them as they landed.

"Why are you here?" asked Bremin, concerned for his old friend.

"Our village isn't protected anymore." Lentoplus panted as he looked back over his shoulder, hoping to see his friend Tern, but he wasn't there. "T'lof and Tern are dead," said Lentoplus. "Tern stayed to avenge T'lof's death."

"I can't believe this," Randle said suddenly since he was caught off guard by the news. "Your village is one of the protected." Then he thought for a moment trying to figure it out.

"If by any chance Avlon somehow found the spells to protect the western villages, then all hope is lost, but what if …" and a thought came to the druid, which made him smile ruefully. Looking back at his new allies, he knew that the chances of succeeding were much better.

"I have to do a few things before we go." Randle announced keeping his thoughts to himself before he could voice them. He wasn't sure if it would work or not but he had to try.

"Bremin, we need more supplies for these two. Since we're all going to Tellet?" The elves and the healed halfling nodded in reply.

"Let's do it," Lentoplus said with grim enthusiasm, and then went over to get a lot more water bottles. None of them knew what the druid was planning, but what ever it was, they would follow him to stop this madness at whatever cost.

CHAPTER TWO

As the sound of pickaxes hit rock hard stone, two dwarves looked at each as they worked; one of them smiled, and then glanced at the nearby guards and their fellow comrades.

"Trolls," Gandis whispered harshly, since his skin was as tough as leather just like his brother's. "I hate them." His twin brother nodded in agreement. They went back to work so the guards would not notice their conversation.

"DON'T DIG THERE," Jandis yelled hoping to catch the attention of one of the troll guards who had come over to inspect the trouble.

"This is my hole," Gandis said angrily, as he held his pickaxe at the ready

"No, it's mine," claimed Jandis as he smashed is pickaxe onto a stone. It broke from the impact, as did several other rocks.

"You two stop it," the giant troll commanded but they ignored him, waiting out for their chance to strike.

"It's mine," Gandis hissed angrily, putting up a good act to distract the guard. The guard came over, as did two others, since they had heard the argument as well.

"Is not," Jandis hissed back then they raised their pickaxes. The troll guard stepped up to them just a couple of inches away. Both swung at the same moment, catching the troll off guard as the two axes plunged into the troll's body, which killed him instantly.

The two watched the huge troll fall to the ground, hard.

Jandis dropped his pickaxe as he picked went over to the now dead body, he yanked the keys off the belt; he retrieved his pickaxe that he dropped and unlocked both of their handcuffs. Then he tossed the keys to another dwarf, who, in turn, unlocked himself and several others.

Gandis and Jandis ran deeper into the mountain hoping to find an escape route. It seemed like hours, but it was minutes until they gave up running. Dwarves were everywhere, unchained and killing their would-be slavers. Trolls and Orcs fell all about them. The twin dwarves jumped over a dead troll

The two rounded a corner a second later as they walked over to the Nortel that was chained to the wall.

"We're freeing you," Jandis told the elf-like creature that towered over them, its gray skin looking black in the darkness. His pickaxe hit the chain. It didn't break, but there was a sound of it cracking under the impact.

"In your debt," it spoke harshly, then swiped at the oncoming gnomes with it's free hand, which careened into the wall, killing them all. The huge creature howled a war cry.

The mountain was in chaos; every slave was fighting. They needed to be free and so they fought their slavers, killing hundreds or maybe thousands of their vast enemy that didn't stop coming. Every where you looked, Orcs, gnomes, and trolls smashed into their slaves, but this only urged the Dwarves even more. They fought to be free; their hope had been restored.

The other three creatures snapped their chains without

any pain while the rush of their captors came toward them.

The twins entered another chamber and saw an old friend. "Tundra!" Gandis exclaimed while Jandis broke the chain that held their elven friend and four other dwarves. Six Orcs rushed into the small room only to meet the huge creature's hands, which slammed them into the rock wall, which dazed them. It howled in fury, two no three dwarves smashed their tools into the Orc's hide.

"There's no way out," Jandis said, but just then, another Orc was slammed into a corner of the wall, which gave way from the impact, and they heard the rocks hit water.

"We're saved!" Gandis, shouted out for all to hear. He raced across and dropped through the hole, as did several others. Jandis looked over his shoulder to see the big creatures battle their enemies.

"We'll be back," he yelled, and then dropped into the cold water that carried them for miles upon miles down the river that led to a vast city known as Cupnee.

"The dwarves are escaping," an Orc shouted in fury and then turned, only to be bashed over the head with the backside of and axe, but he swiped the dwarf away as if it were a fly.

"Zentel," he called out, "the dwarves are escaping!"

His boss snarled at him. "I can see that, nimrod," he said, as he killed a dwarf with his sword. Zentel the troll was angry at the situation. "Get them back," he ordered. His subordinate looked disheartened.

"Four hundred have escaped. We'll never get them back," the Orc said dejectedly.

"No one questions my command," snapped Zentel. "No matter what, I will get them back." He raised his sword and cut him down. "I want those dwarves back," he yelled

"Yes, sir," said a troll and ran toward the portal room that lay off to the left of the chamber.

Placing his hand on the shiny orb in the middle of the portal room, the troll saw a green face appear in its surface.

"Why have you called me?" the insane Tekker asked not willing to discuss this, but he had to.

"We've lost over four hundred dwarves," the troll informed his master.

The Tekker didn't look pleased by the news.

"I will send someone. Avlon out," Avlon said.

Avlon stood quietly in his chamber since he found peaceful thoughts that way. He liked the idea of silence, but he hated that things had been going wrong lately.

A lone figure stood behind him in the shadows of the chamber.

"You summoned me," the figure said not willing to come into the light.

"Indeed, I have a chore for you. I have lost over four hundred dwarves, which were in Hell Mountain. Return them and I'll give you two hundred gold coins."

"It'll be my pleasure," the man said confidently then walked out of the chamber, leaving Avlon Klynn to his thoughts. What the man did not know was that Avlon knew that the young man would betray him one day just like the others over the years. He was binding his time with this human since he was different than the others; he sensed something was different about the dwarf hunter of which he couldn't place his finger on it.

Picking up a bucket each, the two humans dipped their buckets into the lake to get some water. The shoulder length blond-haired man grinned as he looked over at his friend. Jack smiled back; his was brown and was closely cut as he spilled water over himself.

"Better not waste water," his friend commented. Then, he heard a noise in the lake which drew their attention. "You hear that?"

"Sounds to me like it's coming from over there," Jack said as he pointed toward the mouth of the river. They both ran over with their buckets in hand, water sloshed all over their feet as rushed over as the two of them saw several forms in the water.

Ten small forms emerged from the lake a moment later, splashing water all about them, happy that they were free at last.

"Do you need any help?" Jack offered not sure why he was smiling faintly.

"YIPPPY!" the dwarves yelled in delight, and then realized that two human beings had spoken to them.

"I'll be a human's uncle," the dwarf exclaimed. "'Bout time some one offered us help." Then he noticed that other humans were looking their way. A broad grin engulfed the dwarves as they realized that they were in a city.

"Where are we?" Gandis asked in awe of the size of the city.

"You're in Cupnee," Reid said, spotting a lot more dwarves coming over to them.

"My brothers and I request shelter for a few nights," Jandis said. He gazed at the sight of the city; he could see the people scurry about, buying things to survive or to wear. It was enormous; the buildings were three stories high or bigger. All was man made, even the buildings themselves. Several Inns could be seen, as he looked down the street. He couldn't read the signs since they were too far way. To his left, he could see several stores, he noted. One sold baked goods; another sold shoes and clothes.

People laughed or conversed as they noticed the rather large group of dwarves.

To his right, Jandis smiled since he now saw a few pubs. All had funny names, he noted as long they had good ale, he thought. His brother conversed with the two humans. All Jandis wanted to do was to explore the vast city. He looked high over the city buildings seeing a castle that lay in the center. Birds flew by, happy, as were the humans.

I bet they're spoiled rotten, Jandis thought, and thought he did about the riches they would have to plunder in this great city. A few men looked his way who did not seem happy to see them. His brother caught his attention at last as Jack nodded.

"I'll see what we can do for you? How many are there?" he asked as he tried to count the dwarves by himself.

"'Bout four hundred and fifty dwarves and fifty elves, depending on how many make it out alive," the dwarf told him, wiping his wet hair away with his right hand. The two looked surprised at the number.

"We'll do what we can," Jack said as he smiled warmly and left in a hurry.

Jandis whispered to his brother, pointing toward the pub off to their right. Gandis laughed heartedly liking the idea. They started to move that way only to be stopped by a peddler. Gandis held out a gold coin and smiled warmly.

"Buy anything you want," Gandis said, pleased to see the man happy as he walked away from them. Entering the pub a second later, heads all looked their way, then went back to conversing with each other.

"Have a seat," a waitress said as she walked over them,

being pleasant and friendly with them. Jandis liked the sight of her since she was beautiful in her own way.

Grabbing a chair each, the two dwarves sat down and ordered them selves some ale, before anything else happened to them. She turned and walked away as a soldier came walking up to them.

"I'm Mantel, a soldier of Darren's army. I wish you welcome to our great city, please visit him at the castle even at your leisure," Mantel Veronf said. Jandis looked up at the man. You could tell he liked to drink, since his nose was big as well as his belly. He shifted slightly as he gazed at the two dwarves that stared back at him, he became nervous so he left the two to ponder if they should go up to the castle.

"Should we?" Gandis said, pondering over their thoughts on the matter as his twin brother nodded, seeing the waitress walk over to them with their drinks.

"No one else will. Besides we do have to make an example," Jandis said as the drinks were put on the table. Both drank the ale in one shot which surprised the waitress, both of them stood up suddenly causing their chairs to crash against the floor, Gandis laid down two gold coins on the table then left the pub.

Entering into the throne room an hour later, Gandis and his brother Jandis studied the grand room pictures lined the walls, kings and queens long forgotten. A picture hung over the throne, the last king who held the vast army of the west. His nose wasn't long, it was short, and his eyes were kind but hardened by hard times.

"Beautiful, isn't it?" a voice said behind them. The two dwarves turned to see the speaker, who looked like a peddler with a dark goatee. His lips were in a frown; he held a strong presence of a strong leader. His hair was brown in color which is cut short, enough so his ears could be seen. He held a dark presence, but the two dwarves didn't seem too noticed since he had a gentle smile.

"I'm Darren, leader and head of this city," he said confidently. "I'm told that you and your people have traveled a long way, from Hell Mountain. That I heard."

Darren knew well that Hell Mountain was one of the many strongholds for thousands of slaves. The others were scattered over the land known as Twilight. Upper Point consisted of six hundred square miles and had at least six strongholds. Then, in the East Side Edge, over ten thousand dwarves were used as slaves. Anywhere you went, you had to be sure that your company of travelers did not contain traitors or spies.

The two nodded as they looked at Darren, surprised by the confidence of the man.

"It's amazing that you survived the journey since there are monsters in the underground river," Darren said as the two smiled at him.

"Monsters no more, sir," Jandis murmured. Then his twin brother introduced them.

As the two turned to leave the chamber, Darren stopped them with a stare.

"I'm willing to help you free your people," Darren said, which caught them off guard.

Jandis started to jump up and down in glee while his older brother turned to look at the human not sure to trust him at all.

"You're offering to help us?" Gandis couldn't believe his luck. He knew it was too good to be true. What does this man want in return? Gandis thought, enslavement or something else all together?

"We need to be free," Darren informed them as if he could read the dwarf's mind and smiled at the brother of the two dwarves. "You look worried. Don't you trust me?"

Gandis nodded his head sheepishly and said aloud with confidence.

"But we're all slaves or prisoners of Avlon." He narrowed his eyes as he said the name.

CHAPTER THREE

For two days straight, Randle and the others hadn't encountered any resistance from their enemies, but they knew it would come one way or another. Settling down for lunch as Lentoplus sat by a tree, Lentoplus thought he heard a crackle in the grass a few yards away.

"Who's there?" he called out hoping that it wasn't an Orc patrol. His heart skipped a beat, frightened that he might have alerted the enemy to their location. Two Elvish heads popped up from the tall grass that surrounded them, and he sighed with relief.

"Lentoplus, is that you?" one of the elves said which had shoulder length hair each had golden hair, as the two rushed over and stopped before they collided with him. Both were amazed to see their comrade in arms.

"It is you!" Tunalun exclaimed and hugged Lentoplus since he hadn't seen him in many a year. The druid and the halfling looked slightly surprised that the elf knew them. He cleared his throat hoping to grab their attention. Lentoplus looked back at his traveling companions.

"These are my older brothers, Prince Tunalun and that's Talin." Bremin said introducing his brothers to the druid and the halfling.

"Where's Tern and T'lof?" the Prince asked. Silence

followed the question. The two new arrivals noticed the sadness in Lent's stance as he looked down at the ground, not really knowing what was plaguing his mind

Randle the druid blurted out in surprise,

"By Mercul, Your brothers?" he said with disbelief as he shook his head in. "Tunalun is the Prince. How can he be your brother, Lent?"

Talin turned his head slightly to the druid and smiled warmly to him since he knew of the druid that stood before him as he tried to explain.

"Our father found out that our mother had an affair with King Landfield. The Third Lent here is Tunalun's half brother," said Talin.

Zek smiled at the situation, amazed that an elf could be someone's lover he never figured that an elf could be attracted to a human but it seemed so since Zek could see there was a slight difference in appearance.

"After ten years of my life with the royal family," Lent explained, "I found out I wasn't wanted within the Royal circle, so I ran away from home. For a while I lived off the land until a kind human family in the mountainside decided to help raise me." He thought a moment. "How's dad by the way?" he wondered with curiosity. .

"He's fine," Tunalun replied, then turned his attention to the druid, a fox scurried past them not willing to sink of human flesh. "Two of our villages have been attack leaving no one to find," Tunalun explained.

Randle looked puzzled. He tried to figure out how Avlon had bypassed his magic, yet it didn't come to him.

"None?" Randle dared to ask slightly upset about the situation

"Not one, but I did hear that all villages near Cupnee have been evacuated," the Prince stated, which helped a little to ease the druids' reaction. Something was up. Why had Avlon sought out to destroy their homes? It just didn't make sense. Looking about him as he thought, a flock of birds soared past them, as if they were flying away from an enemy.

"They could have escaped unnoticed," Randle said, trying to bring some hope to the surface.

"You're right, of course. We usually leave the villages when there is an invading force is near by," said Tunalun glad that Randle had thought about that.

Strolling through a meadow some time later, the travelers noticed the far off city of Cupnee; some of the buildings could be seen from the other side of the forest that lay before them. Randle looked to his right seeing another far off city, this one was a bit more difficult to see since it was so far away. It was the city of Tellet.

"That's Odd," Randle said, as he pointed to the nearby forest with his right hand. "Somebody is in the forbidden forest."

A high horrid screech filled the late morning air.

"Cover your ears," Randle warned his group. As they did, they noticed a horde of trolls and gnomes rushing out of the forest all of them had the look of terror plastered on their faces as if a monster had spooked them. A grayish creature leaped out of the woods, it was eight feet tall and it landed on top of two giant trolls. The others fled for their lives. They scurried away trying to stay away from the creature but it was no good. As the nortel swiped at them like flies. Flowers and grass were ruined by the tangled, dead bodies.

"A nortel!" Randle went on to explain not surprised to see the creature at all, it laid havoc on the trolls and gnomes as the creature killed them all. Randle knew that the elf like creature was friendly if you left them alone. As Talin raised his bow, Talin felt the druid's hand stop him before he could do anything. "No," the druid commanded. "He's protecting his home from invaders. He won't hurt us, only the trolls,"

The group watched in amazement at the scene before them. The group shuddered as the nortel killed the last of the trolls with its bare hands. They had never witnessed the fury of a nortel before since they had never seen one before.

The nortel settled its sight on the group as it decided to head for them. Bremin studied the features of the creature as it approached them, a long narrow face with pointed ears. Much like an elf, he thought, and he now noticed that the creature wasn't grey, but greenish grey.

"You there," the Nortel said in common, "could have helped me fight this small army."

The group stared at the creature puzzled since they were wondering where it had learned their language.

"It's not safe here. Barehaven will admit you," the giant creature told them as he walked a few steps toward the group, which cowered in fear, but it then ushered them to follow. "If you are going to Cupnee, you might as well use the forest. It is the faster way," it told them.

"We're going to Tellet first, we have business there" said Randle as he wiped off some grass since the nortel was covered in it.

The group started to follow it. Now alongside the huge creature, Arcan shook his head still puzzled by it. He was curious.

"So, how did you learn to speak common?" Randle asked, no longer afraid of the creature. He inched a spot on the lower half of his back. The creature smiled, but it looked more like a snarl.

"No one enter forest, for long time, but human and elves voices are heard. For over two hundred years, we listened, and then the Prophecy came true when the human was found." It informed them which Randle became mildly interested at the words prophecy and human. What did the creature mean by those words and how did they find this human? He cleared his throat.

"I know of your people. I read of them at Telmar where some of the other druids are. I read all about your history."

The nortel listened, eager to hear what the druid had to say.

"It is said that over two thousand years ago, your race was born to this planet."

The creature nodded in agreement.

"That's right. We are one of the six races, an off shoot of the elves like the Tenal or the Sover." The nortel then added after he couched, "As for the other two races of elves, we have no idea where they are or where they are hiding."

The druid had heard of the other races of the elves and visited them. The Tenal welcomed him as a fighter since they are warriors at heart and are spiritual, too since they worshiped a goddess of extreme power. The Sover preferred to be left alone, in the distant mountains of the North, but since Avlon controlled all of the lands, they were just as captive as everyone else.

The group and the huge creature entered the lush forest a second later.

CHAPTER FOUR

Crouching behind a bush, Gandis noted the swarm of trolls and gnomes in the area. They hid behind some bushes so not to be seen. A bunch of trees was on Reid's right. This blocked the enemies' path.

"They must be looking for us," Gandis said to Reid, the human soldier, which was on his right as he picked up a fallen leaf and studied it. He tossed it away, not wishing to have it any more.

"I take it that those were your slave masters," Reid said, observing the enemy to see what they were doing, "forcing you and your race to do things you didn't want to do."

Gandis nodded at the statement; he knew it was time to attack. An arrow flew into the air, and the gnomes in the front died right away, not knowing what had hit them since they were looking at the grass as if they were trying to pick up any signs of prints. Rushing out into the field with his pickaxe as a weapon, Gandis could see his brother killing a troll. As another troll loomed over him a second later, he clutched his pickaxe with his two hands he swung his blade at the troll's leg it hit as the creature cried out in pain as the blade sliced into its flesh.

"DIE!" Gandis yelled at the top of his voice as his

blood rage took over but before Gandis knew it, the fight was over. "What happened?" He was astonished at the sight of the enemy, which lay dead, scattered in the field for any to see. He and a few others were the only ones that did not get to kill to many of the Trolls or Orcs.

"It was only a small troop," Jack said as he put his sword away, unsympathetic to their own victory. Darren noticed that Jack was unsympathetic but he dismissed it for now.

"We have a long journey ahead of us, and we'd better get going," Darren said to everyone as he came out of hiding from a nearby bush.

"Gandis, Jack. I want the two of you to scout ahead," Darren suggested then he turned to look at the other two. "Reid, Jandis, I want you two to cover their rear."

The four nodded, understanding their assignments. Jandis stopped for a brief moment before leaving. "Sir?" as he caught Darren's attention.

"Yes, Jandis what is it?" said Darren, eager to hear what Jandis had to say.

"Your troop should call you commander," commented Jandis. "Or better yet they should call you King."

Darren smiled at the thought as he placed his right hand on the dwarf's shoulder.

"Thank you for the suggestion I do like the good idea." He replied, liking the thought, but he knew that was not his path. He had not been raised in Cupnee, so he could not be King. Darren had hidden his past well, no one knew where he came from since it was better for him to keep so little friends. He watched the four leave the area. Slowly and carefully, the four searched for more enemies for what seemed like hours. Finally, Reid noticed something ahead of them.

"I'll be right back," Reid said to his friends as he dashed off to see what lay ahead of them but they followed after him anyway.

Hiding behind some bushes, trying to stay clear of the field, Reid noticed several gnome bodies were all scattered about as if a battle had taken place.

"Dear God," he whispered, not believing the scene before him. Someone or something had done battle here.

"Whoever did this will really piss off Avlon," Reid said, and he then entered the field hoping that nothing was still alive as he noticed on the ground, several feet away, a single arrow shaft, the only one in the area. Picking it up with his fingers, he could tell it had not been fired at all since it had no markings from striking of flesh or dirt or wood. Someone had dropped it. Looking at the bodies again, he now noticed that several of the gnomes had their heads had been bashed into their bodies. "That had to have hurt," he said to himself. As he touched his neck, he breathed though his mouth so he wouldn't chock from the smell of the dead. Then he turned around only to see the other three staring at the dead bodies. "I found this arrow. Can't tell where it's from."

Walking toward the human, Jandis grabbed at the arrow and studied it carefully.

"It's elven," Jandis told Reid, who in turn looked surprised by the statement.

Gandis looked up at him and then sniffed the air as if he were an elf. He studied the grass and stared off into the forbidden Forest,

"The elves went that way," Gandis said as he pointed toward the forbidden forest. The others looked at the wooded area. All of them were surprised by the announcement.

"No one dares to go in there," Reid said surprised.

"Why not?" Jandis said, determined to go into the forest no matter what anyone would say to him. The tips of his worn out boots touched a dead body, but he didn't care.

"It's forbidden," Reid told him. He scratched his head. "Unless they were invited."

"Who cares?" Jack said sharply. "The dwarves need our help." He strode ahead.

"What's bugging him?" Gandis questioned with a slight smile as they followed.

Reid replied soberly as he considered of telling him,

"He lost a brother years ago, but Jack tells a tale of a great green monster that killed him."

Jandis shot a look at his brother. They both knew and had seen the species they had helped in the escape. However, it sounded strangely off, as if Jack's tale was somewhat strange.

"Nortels were peaceful creatures, not killers," said Jandis as he made a point. "Are you sure it was one of them?" he questioned.

"Not really," Reid replied and let the matter drop as if it never happened.

"Reid, Jack," Gandis said, "I have something important to do. I'll catch you up later."

The two humans looked at him and nodded.

"Go ahead, Gandis," Reid said as he watched the dwarf heading toward the forbidden forest. "You better go after him, Jack. Jandis and I can take care of each other."

Jack looked back at him, displeased by the sound of the suggestion.

"We all go then," Jack replied defeated since he was hoping to get away from the area. The memory had haunted him for a long time, he felt alone and afraid that something might happen to him as well. His mind wondered he knew he was within the service of Brail which is a great demon; he had to think about his actions since he has been betraying Darren for the past two years.

Walking at a steady pace, Gandis heard the other three follow him.

"We're helping you," Reid stated, but the dwarf shook his head displeased by the suggestion.

"I think it would be better if we stayed together," Jack insisted hoping to get back to the task at hand.

"What about the army?" Gandis asked him, not willing to hear the answer.

Jack glanced about them as he studied their faces.

"You're right. Jandis and I will scout ahead for them while you two do whatever is so important," Reid insisted, as he patted his traveling bag.

Gandis looked at his brother and smiled faintly, "May Random look over you, Jandis." Said Gandis to his twin brother as he looked away and walked further into the forest.

"What's this you have to do?" Jack asked as he caught up with the dwarf easily. Gandis didn't reply right away. Finally, he answered,

"It has to do with the Nortels," Gandis replied, not willing to tell the human what it was about. He had to tell them something important.

Jack looked worried and angry at the thought. "They're killers, plain and simple," Jack said coldly.

"No, you've got it all wrong. Nortels are just misled," Gandis told him.

Jack went quiet with blind hatred.

For a mile and a half as they trekked through the forest,

both Jack and Gandis didn't speak a word to each other. As they neared a small clearing that hung off to their left. The dwarf was listening for trouble and could see much better than any human could. He placed his hand out to stop his human friend.

"What is that noise?" Jack asked, startled by the gesture.

"Shhh," Gandis put a finger to his lips so he could hear and then sniffed the air as if he were a dog; he detected the elven party just ahead, which wasn't too far ahead.

Odd, he thought, *it smells as if we're on top of them.* Then, as he moved a foot, Jack called out a warning.

"Don't move!"

Gandis looked worried for a change as he took a breath.

"You've been following the elves toward Barehaven, haven't you?" Jack said, detecting the truth for once. The red haired, broad nosed, and tough skinned dwarf nodded.

"How did you know?" Gandis replied in a huff.

Jack bent down to study the broken twigs.

"See here? These are elf markings, and those," he pointed, "are Nortel marks."

Gandis called out, "It's all right. We're friends."

The group of eight got up from their hiding places. A Nortel made himself known. As he breathed out, his stomach made him visible from behind a tree. They could look like they weren't there at all.

"Jack is that you?" the druid said, and then smiled at the youth. The two clasped hands

"Randle, it's been a long time," Jack said with a smile to see a good friend of his father's.

As Randle studied the dwarf up and down he had a feeling there was more than met the eye since he had never known a dwarf to wander the land.

"I thought the dwarves were all slaves," Randle said out of hand, trying no to be rude.

"That's a long story, druid. I'm Gandis by the way," Gandis said as he introduced himself. He looked at the nortel as he sized him up and down. "Your brothers gave me a message before I escaped."

The nortel waited for his message, eager to hear what the dwarf had to say.

"That is?" The nortel urged too eager for his own good.

"Unite with your cousins and the humans," Gandis said. "We must destroy Hell Mountain at all costs. The human army and we dwarves are on our way now. If we destroy Hell Mountain, it will be a small victory for our side."

The nortel liked the idea as he pondered the thought of a free land once more; he smiled at last which startled the group of people. Gandis waited for a reply as the Nortel scratched its head; he didn't say anything as he felt like exploding since it was taking to long.

"I must take this to the others, they will know more than me. I'm just a soldier to you, my commander will make that decision" said the nortel as it paused for a moment. "We're not far from Barehaven. It's only a half mile that way." He pointed southwest and thought fast. "I can get there in five minutes, but if I stay with you, it will take half an hour. I'll meet you there, okay?"

The nortel didn't waste any time. The group was startled by the speed of the beast as it ran away; it was very silent as it ran.

Gandis smiled as the others looked at him, puzzled and surprised that a dwarf had that effect on anybody or anything. Arcan smiled weakly at the dwarf then turned slightly to regard the druid as it now focused its gaze onto him.

"Let's go. We'd better hurry. Sounds to me that we have important business ahead of us," Randle remarked, as he placed his hands by his side. A chipmunk hopped onto his shoulder, took a piece of a leaf off his shoulder, and leaped off.

After walking for half an hour, which seemed like hours, Randle and the others were greeted by another nortel, which was slightly taller as the other one, but for some reason, the druid could tell that this one had more fat on him. Its narrow eyes looked at them, as it studied the group before him. It opened its mouth to speak.

"B'lenton, told us to expect you," the nortel told them as he ushered them into town with a gesture of his hand.

The humans and dwarf gazed at the sight before them, the village was beautiful to look at, and a few stalls lay ahead of them selling all sorts of things. The houses were made from wood, just like the elves' homes. In the center of the small village, four spruce trees could be seen as small nortel children studied the flowers under them. Just on the other side of the village a single temple was open to the air; a few Nortel sat as they worshiped their god, Findor the Drangery.

"We will give you food and supplies for your journey ahead," the nortel said as he smiled at them, which looked more like a snarl. The druid nodded his head as he thanked the creature and his hospitality.

"Kind of you and your people to do this," Randle said grateful for a kind gesture.

"It's our pleasure to help since you're going to Tellet,"

the nortel replied.

The druid thought for a moment and then said what was on his mind.

"How did you know that we were going there?" he questioned not sure if he wanted to hear the answer.

"It has been foretold. The Prophecies state that an important druid will bring down Avlon Klynn. That much we have read so far. As of your passage through our forest, we will all ways be glad to grant you passage. As for Cupnee, don't bother. Darren knows of the threat," the nortel said, eager to tell them more if they asked.

The druid and the others looked at each other. Randle suddenly seemed interested in the subject of the prophecies and then asked where the library was. Entering a nearby building, right away, the druid started to look for the book in the library.

"Can I help you?" A voice asked from behind the seven foot druid as he rifled through a few books that intrigued him further.

"I was told you had a few books on Prophecies."

The owner nodded as he urged the druid to follow him. "I do. Please step this way." He led the druid to the back where there didn't appear to be any books. However, resting on a table were two covered books, which the druid noticed that had odd-looking shapes. Picking up the tablecloth that hid both the books from sight, the owner started to walk back to him. "If you want to read, go right ahead. If not, you can pay for them."

The druid picked up both of the books.

"I'll pay for them," Randle insisted and the nortel smiled.

Leaving the library/store a moment later, he noticed a human male in the market, which seemed odd to him since he was the only human in the village beside him and the rest of his group. He was handing over food and drink to the locals. Walking over to him Randle noticed that he stood about five feet six inches; his brown hair was neatly cut short as the druid made his approach noticeable.

"What can I do for you stranger?" asked the stallholder.

"Do you have any orange juice?" Randle asked the young man, as he looked around. It wasn't busy, but at least it was a steady pace for the human.

"I do," the young male said as he reached his hand onto the table, which contained several containers of different kinds of juice. He handed Arcan a full glass, after he poured it.

"How did you get here?" Randle wanted to know as he sipped the juice since he was eager to hear the tale.

"When I was ten, I was playing with my brother Jack, but I tripped and stumbled into this forest and was attacked by three gnomes. B'lenton came out and killed them. After that, I couldn't find my brother, so I followed the nortel here, and he helped raised me."

The druid had a thought. He suspected that Jack was up to something though he needed proof of what it was. Encountering this young man, Arcan had a feeling that he was supposed to join them in their quest.

"My friends and I are going to Tellet. Would you like to join us?"

The man shook his head, not sure if he should go or not. Bobby knew leaving wasn't the right thing since he would be abandoning his post. He looked over his shoulder to see his boss walk toward them. The nortel spoke to the boy.

"Go with the druid, Bobby."

Randle looked up at the nortel and smiled warmly at the thought. "It's time you went back to the human world," the nortel said. "My kind must move on. This forest is no longer safe for us; there have been too many attacks lately."

Bobby turned back to stare at the druid.

"It looks like I'm coming with you and your troop after all," and then he placed another cup in the druid's hand.

After drinking the juice, the two passed several stalls along the way, neither the druid nor Bobby spoke, but Randle had learned of the separation some time ago when one of his sons came to visit him at the druid keep.

"Guys," the druid got their attention. "Bob here is joining us."

Jack stared at him blankly. He recognized his own brother; Jack didn't know what he felt at first.

"Bobby?" Jack said, surprised to see his long lost brother and studied his face for a better look. "Dear God," he uttered as his face went pale. "You're alive."

"Who are you?" Bob asked not knowing who was talking to him. He didn't recognize his own brother since it had been years the last time either saw each other.

"Bobby, it's me. Jack," but the man before him looked puzzled. "Don't you remember your own brother?"

Bobby jerked with a start as a smile formed on his face. He looked at his brother now remembering him for the first time. "Jack. How are you, brother? And where is Reid?" overwhelmed to see his own brother as the two hugged. Randle smiled at the mention of one of his sons, he had never been there for either of them but at least the families the two went to were nice to them.

"Okay," Gandis said, slightly puzzled "Now we have a new member," and then thought a moment. *What is Randle thinking? Whatever it is, it had better be good.*

As Jandis peered over the edge of a small hill carefully, he could see another hunting party of trolls and gnomes.

"Boy, they sure don't give up," exclaimed Reid as he reached behind him to get something.

"Quiet," Jandis whispered then peered over the edge again and saw an Orc walking over with a bag that moved around that hang over his shoulder.

"Ark, la sin!" it bellowed, and then dropped it to the ground as a female cried out.

"Someone's in that bag," said Reid since he was concerned for the female's safety. "We've got to rescue whoever is in it." He pulled out a bow and arrow which was the same size of his hand.

Jandis looked over at him as he realized what the human was about to do since he was armed.

"Are you nuts or what? If you fire, we could be detected," Jandis whispered harshly.

"I know what I'm doing," Reid assured the dwarf as he fired the single shot.

The dwarf watched with horror as the tiny arrow hit the ground in the middle of the enemy camp. The whole camp jumped to attention, ready to do battle, each and every Orc and gnome held their weapons at the ready only to fall to the ground, asleep a second later.

"What was that?" Jandis asked in wonderment.

"Sleeping gas," Reid told him with a smirk as he got to his feet and leapt down into the enemy camp without a single thought, the dwarf following behind him. "They will be asleep for hours, while we'll be long gone."

He walked over to the bag. Opening it, the two were shocked to see a young elven girl asleep. Bending down,

Reid placed some smelling salts under her nose to wake her.

Blinking rapidly, she stared at the two, amazed that she had been rescued. She opened her mouth to take a yawn as she sized the human up and down.

"Where am I?" she asked as Reid helped her to her feet as she now noticed the dwarf for the first time.

"A dwarf?" she muttered in mock contempt and then looked at her rescuer again. "Oh, my," she said as she was helped to her feet, she glanced into his eyes. "You've got beautiful eyes, handsome," she told him flirting with the human, which caused Reid to blush. He found it flattering as his pride swelled up at the thought. "Thanks for getting me out of that bag. It smelled really bad in there."

Reid didn't know what to say or do, but the dwarf smiled up at her.

"Tell me something," the elf said to him.

He nodded, "What would you like to know?"

She rolled her eyes at him. "Are you two going to Hell Mountain?"

The two looked at each other, not sure what to tell her. Jandis was not willing to tell her anything, but he heard Reid said.

"Yes," Reid admitted.

"No," Jandis corrected. "We will probably go that way." Pointing off in another direction, which led to Hill Hide Manor, which was a village that had a great reputation for being a heroes' village.

Reid couldn't take his eyes off her beauty.

The elf studied the two of them, since she had no idea what they were trying to do.

"Are you done joking around?" She thought the matter over and looked confused. "Can you tell me then why you're going?"

"I, and many others of my brethren, escaped the mountain. We're with a great army who are going to free the others," Jandis informed her telling her the truth.

"Just the two of you and the escaped dwarves?" she asked, shaking her head in pity.

"No, four hundred dwarves and a human army," Reid said as he saw her flinch at the thought, which caused him to be alarmed.

Looking at the two of them, the elven lady wondered, *I could tip the scale here and now, but let's find out more about this so-called army.* She smiled at the two. *I wonder, who is their leader?* She dared to ask. *No,* she thought; *better to find out by meeting him or her. These two don't know who I am.*

She placed her right hand on Reid's shoulder and winked, "We'd better get going," she suggested, and the three left the sleeping party behind.

Staying within the shadows so not to be seen, Shannon watched a single dwarf from a distance then noticed that he wasn't alone. He watched the group emerge from some bushes and then he noticed the druid.

"Randle," he whispered, "I should have known." He sneered at the thought, and then noticed another group coming. *Wait just a minute,* he thought. *Snit, I'm wrong.*

"Well, look what we have here?" a voice said from behind him. Turning towards the voice, Shannon straightened, knowing it wasn't Arcan at all, but his own brother who was a year older.

His eyes narrowed at his brother; Shannon did not like to be tricked. But at least he was glade to his older brother.

"So you fooled me, Conner. I don't like to be fooled by

wizards." Shannon said sharply.

"Yet, father was one," replied Conner.

The young man was upset by the thought. "Fliss off," he snapped a bit too angrily.

Conner was nobody's fool, but he and Shannon were blood brothers. He looked back at him since neither of them smiled, both were glade to see each other but it had been years since they had last saw each other.

"Shannon, I found out that you're hunting dwarves for Avlon again. Bad move, by the way. And when did you return from our home country?"

Shannon took a step toward him. His one armored arm hung at his side while the druid hood hung from his neck. His boots, pants, and shirt were like a cobbler's. A small knife hung in a pouch. His eyes where hard and cold. "It's my business wizard, not yours, brother," then added in a much calmer voice, "I arrived back two weeks ago." He turned away.

The wizard searched his thoughts, hoping to gain some idea of what the young man was going through, but he came up empty.

"I avenged for your dead wife" Conner informed his brother who looked at him. Sadness filled his eyes, he turned to leave.

"I've got to go," Shannon said and disappeared into the brush; Conner had delayed him for a purpose. He knew his master was waiting for him. He then looked the way the small group had gone. *I'll halve the time*, Conner thought and disappeared into thin air.

Emerging from a clearing, Shannon studied the area as he noticed a great army of dwarves and humans. "What the--!" He exclaimed and bent down behind a bush so he would not to be seen.

After getting the last of their supplies, Randle and the others had left Barehaven. Randle was on the alert because he had sensed that they were being watched even before arriving at Barehaven. Walking through the forest, Arcan now noticed it was quiet and peaceful.

"I wonder how the evil master was able to deactivate the protected villages." Arcan wondered. Could he have used my nephews?

Bobby glanced quickly at Bremin as he formed a thought. He was wondering if he should tell them.

"A female elf was kidnapped two years ago. After they brainwashed her, she turned evil," Bobby informed his newfound .friends

The druid smiled but was puzzled by the news.

"How the hell do you know that?"

Bobby tripped over a root since he wasn't paying much attention to his surroundings. Randle helped the boy up and noticed the tattoo on the young man's hand, but he didn't say a word. The druid had seen the tattoo once before, but that was long ago and that was someone else all together. *Protector* sprang to his mind but only selected people bore the mark.

"I was helping my girlfriend, Ricla Kenulan, with some of her things--," said Bobby, but Bremin cut him off sharply.

"She's royalty. She would never betray her kind, nor see a mere human."

"I don't care what you think, elf," replied Bob a bit too rudely and he knew it. "I was there when they turned and captured her."

Bremin would not be deterred. "She wouldn't turn on her kind; the fact that you claim she's been turned against us is near imposs…"

"That's enough from the two of you!" Randle shouted, he gained some control over him self before he spoke again. "Avlon has the power to brainwash anyone." Then he gave Bobby a sharp look. "I have seen it happen myself." He started to walk away toward their goal.

Walking away from the enemy, Jandis looked over his shoulder just in case one of the trolls was faking. He then glanced over at Reid.

"What do you reckon?" Jandis whispered to the human.

Reid glanced back at him with a smirk on his face. "I'm getting the feeling that she's using us, but I could be wrong."

"She may turn on us," Jandis said trying to whisper softy so the elf would not hear them.

The two noticed that she looked back at them.

"We'd better be going, don't you think?" Ricla suggested and started to walk way from them and the sleeping party. They let her pass them so that they could see what she would do if she tried to escape. They traveled silently. Jandis welcomed the quietness; he would hear if someone was following them.

After what seemed like a day, Jack noticed something in the distance. "Look." He pointed ahead of them, to see a village half a mile away. He then patted the bag to see if it was full or not, but to his dismay found that the bag slung over his shoulder was quite empty.

"This bag's empty. Jandis, we'd better stop to get more supplies," Reid said, but the dwarf halted in mid-stride and smelled the air, detecting trouble ahead.

Jandis went stiff, and the other two noticed that his

color had drained.

"What's wrong?" Reid wondered, perturbed.

Jandis took a step back.

"Forget the food," he finally said as he moved his eyes to the right, indicating that he needed the human to follow his glance.

Studying the area carefully Reid spotted trouble up ahead. Someone was trying to hide from view, but whoever it was had no idea that the three had noticed him.

"Keep walking," Jandis urged, and the other two intended to do what they were told.

Nearing the bushes, Jandis started to talk. "I wonder where we can rest a while." Then he stepped on a branch deliberately.

"I don't know," Ricla said. "We could rest here, in this nice clearing."

Reid tried to move his legs, but they wouldn't move. A figure emerged from his hiding place and smiled at them.

"Looks to me like a traveling clothes rack," Jandis blurted out as the other two burst out laughing.

Shannon pointed his knife at the dwarf, ready to cut him if the dwarf dared to attack.

"You're coming with me, dwarf," Shannon said, displeased that the dwarf was traveling with a human and an elf. He gazed at the elven princes, then moved his eyes to look at the dwarf once again.

The princess kicked him in the stomach. He dropped his weapon. She picked it up.

"You attacked us with this toy," she uttered contemptuously.

He narrowed his eyes at her and knew she was putting on an act. Shannon could feel the magic coming off her. It might just be the brainwashing that he felt. He looked at the dwarf.

"You're one of the escapees." Shannon proclaimed happy to see that he was right when the dwarf stood straighter than normal.

"Who are you?" Jandis demanded. "And what do you want with me?"

"I'm Shannon Lee," the man informed him. "I heard that over four hundred of your kind escaped from Hell Mountain, and I plan on capturing everyone for the reward Avlon has offered."

Ricla moved away. "Release them, now," she threatened with his own knife, and he blinked, not sure if he heard right since it was out of character for her, lifting the magic that held the two in place.

"There you go," Shannon said to them as the knife vanished from her hand and then appeared in the pouch on the belt. She looked surprised, and yet he smiled back at her. Shannon knew who she was and what she was up to but he also knew that fighting all of them would be risky since it was three to one. "Looks as if I won't get Avlon's reward for capturing you," said Shannon, as he looked at Jandis.

The dwarf stopped a moment and thought of an idea. He didn't want to smile since it would give him away. "You'll get your reward, human" Jandis regarded with a sneer.

His statement caught Ricla and Reid off guard.

CHAPTER FIVE

The sun rose over the field of flowers, as Darren picked up the last of his belongs. He and his army had spent the night, camping under the stars for a change. Darren had forgotten what it was like, but now he remembered. A smile was plastered on his face; he was beginning to enjoy him self. His wife looked at him, as she smiled back.

"We better get going," Darren said to the others of his great army. They looked at him as if he was crazy. Some of them hated camping, but they knew they had a task before them, and the thought of battle pleased them. A hawk perched on a tree branch as several birds sang their little song.

Stepping on a broken piece of wood some time later, Darren peered over the edge of a small hill and noticed a hunting party of trolls and gnomes that was fast asleep on the ground. They had gotten up early to find the enemy, but Darren knew what he was going to do. He gestured to the others to be careful not to wake the enemy, making sure not to make a single sound himself. He noticed movement off to his right. He waved one of his men over, and he pointed to the creature that he had picked to question.

Standing over a single gnome, a soldier held his sword at the creature's neck. It stirred.

"Don't cry out, gnome," Darren warned the creature. "Just tell me. Who was in that bag?"

The gnome looked at the sword at first, which was frightening, then looked at Darren with those pleading eyes he had.

"Woman," the yellow creature told him. "Evil woman."

"What you mean, small thing?" Darren threatened the small creature ready to slice the gnome's throat but the sword stayed where it was.

"We helped her escape," said the gnome. "We were attacked. She be gone from home. We help her we did. Evil master was done with her. She no longer required."

Darren glanced at the soldier that stood beside him, who had a puzzled look, and then looked back at the gnome.

"Who is she?" Darren demanded, as he pressed the sword even tighter than before.

"Elven Princess. Two people rescued her, dwarf and human," the gnome blurted out.

Darren now knew that their mission was in danger; he had heard that Ricla had been taken prisoner some time ago but that was over two years ago.

"They're headed to Small," Darren announced to everyone. It was obvious anyway since they were walking toward it for a day; Darren just voiced it aloud. He then strolled over to another soldier as he made a plan of action with his troops. Then back to the gnome who was frantic, since he didn't want to die. It tried to speak but the man's sword pressed against his wind pipe. No longer being silent, "Kill them!" Darren ordered and plunged his own sword into the neck of the gnome as he looked away from the slaughter. The order had to be done. If it wasn't, the evil

master would learn that an army was on its way to Hell
Mountain to kill his force.

"Ricla," Darren said. "The last Princess." He did not
like the name since it meant betrayal. He noticed his wife
walking up to him and he smiled.

"You called?" Willow asked, and he nodded pleased to
see his wife. For far too long Darren wanted to forget his
past, but this killing only enhanced his memories of his
younger days.

"Go to Tellet with Harry, Dale, and Bruce," he said as
he waved them over. "Tell them that their princess has been
found and that she had been turned to the evil side." Darren
said as he touched her cheek. Their eyes met and she
smiled once again. "Have a safe journey," he murmured.

She nodded with a smile "I will husband, and you,
too." She turned, but he gripped her arm softly. She glanced
back. He leaned over slightly as she leaned into him as the
two kissed.

Nearing the elven city of Tellet, Randle stopped for a
moment; he had seen something in the dirt so he bent down
and touched the ground. In the back of the group, Zek
called out,

"What's going on up there?" and the others looked
back at him. He was not willing to tell the halfling of what
was going on since none of them knew.

"Randle is studying the grass, for some reason," Talin
told him, and then looked over at the druid.

Rushing up to the front, Zek noticed a pile of dirt in the
druid's right hand.

"What the hell are you doing? And why?" Zek wanted
to know as the druid ignored him for now.

Randle let the dirt fall through his fingers so that what

was left was some kind of green stone.

"Spread out," the druid told them as he showed the stone to everyone.

"What is it?" Zek wondered, and the tall man smiled warmly at the young halfling.

"It's an elf stone; usually there are three in total. The green stones are the mind, body, and soul. The blue stones are for the humans, and the red are for a dead race no one knows about," Randle informed the halfling as he regarded him with suspicion still as he fingered the stone with his index finger. Pulling out his book, he flipped it open and he whispered for the first time. The pages flipped fast then stopped in the center of the book. He read the page with mild interest.

Zek nodded at the druid, hoping the druid wouldn't continue.

"Randle," Bremin called him over, "I found the second." He stood up to display a blue gemstone which was between is fingers so the others of his group could see as well.

Lent cried out in pain, and the group rushed over to see what had happened.

"What is it?" Randle sounded worried.

"Someone set a bear trap," Talin said.

The druid looked at the deadly trap.

"Looks bad," he exclaimed.

"Good news is I have the third stone."

He opened Lent's trapped hand slowly so as not to hurt him and took the red elf stone from it.

"Where did you find it?" Talin asked the elf called Lent.

"On that branch," Lent replied as he pointed with his other hand. "It was just sitting there so when I jumped to get it, but I lost my footing and landed on this trap."

"Gandis," Randle called the dwarf over. "We need your help. Can you remove this?"

"I could cut the hand off," Gandis joked as he grabbed for his axe.

Lent went white at the suggestion, and then realized the dwarf was joking when he saw him smile.

"Just get my hand out of this," Lent demanded through gritted teeth. Not caring for the cruel joke "This hurts like hell."

Gandis replied with a sneer, "I'm sure it is, but this is going to hurt a lot more," as he yanked open the two sides with his bare hands.

"AHHHHHH!" yelled Lent so loudly that four human strangers came out from the bushes with their bows at the ready. Lent cradled his right hand as he rolled over in pain.

"Who are you?" one of the humans asked.

"Travelers," Randle informed the strangers, noticing the young man he had met once before. Will stared at him for a second as he shook his head.

"We're hunting for dinner," Will stated, also recognizing the druid since he had encounter him a few years ago, but Randle knew he was lying. He stepped to his right and glanced at Bobby, but the human had no idea what the hundred-year-old druid had in mind.

"Sorry for upsetting you," Randle said without any pity as the   man and began to walk away slowly.

"Ha, you can't take the stones," another man said which had a goatee and a closely cut blond hair.

"Just watch me," Randle shot back, slightly angry with his young friend and the others watched as the druid walked away. William let loose an arrow. As it flew through the air, the tall druid reached up in time as the arrow tip passed his hand, as he gripped it.

The hunter looked surprised, and his own troop just stared at him as if Arcan had done an unearthly trick. Will took a few steps toward him trying not to smile, but intended to fend for himself.

"I'm taking the elf stones," the druid repeated.

The hunter shook his head, stunned and confused.

"By the way, young man, where did you get these?" Randle asked with wonder calmly trying not to indicate that he knew William at all.

William stared at the stones for a time unable to reply at first. He just stared at the gem stones taking note as Randle showed them.

"I-I got them from a gnome salesman. He told me that deer liked shiny objects." Then William realized the truth of the matter, as took a step back. "That dirty rotten gnome." He turned on his heels and snarled, "Zentel, we're going after that little thief," and the group of humans disappeared into the bushes.

Glancing at the others, the druid noticed it was nearing the end of the day.

"When we get to Tellet, it will be dark," he announced and the nine of them started to walk the last leg of their journey for the day.

Seeing the sunset as the group entered the vast city of Tellet, the druid noticed that the halfling was surprised by the size of the city. Randle didn't say anything for the moment as he let him gaze about.

"Lent, Zek, you're with me," Randle told them and the two stepped forward. As they walked together, Zek looked at the tall buildings that towered over them on both sides of the street. People scurried about before the stores closed for the night. Others walked with loved ones or in groups.

Some went into pubs for a few drinks and to have a good time. They passed the pub; the sign said Tolken's song. A few trees could be seen, but not well since it was dark.

As they strolled over to the Zelner's house, which lay in the center of the vast city. At least the druid knew where to go. He raised his hand to knock on the door, but he didn't get a chance since the door opened.

"Come in," the chief welcomed them and shook the druid's hand. "It's been along time, old friend." The two smiled, and then hugged quickly since they were happy to see each other.

"Zelner," Randle said to the chief, "this is Zek, and this is Lent," The two nodded at the elf chief that stood before them.

"Please have a seat," he offered them, and they all sat down in the elven chairs.

"Did you hear the news, Arcan?" Zelner said and the druid looked puzzled.

"What news is this?" Randle said, unsure what the news was or where it came from.

Zelner now realized that the druid might not know of what had happened in the past few days.

"A friend of mine came to me today, Randle. She told me that Cupnee had some visitors a few days ago. Dwarves they were. They escaped from Hell Mountain. They had help from the humans with them. Something like three to four hundred were freed from that awful mountain. I've sent troops to help," Zelner said then added as a remark, "You do remember Page Litheart."

Randle smiled, remembering the human female that had helped them long ago. The three looked pleasantly surprised, although the druid and the other two already knew of the dwarves' escape.

"A dwarf is traveling with us," Randle told his old friend. "He told us about the escape and the alliance between the two. It's good you're helping out," and he smiled once more at his friend, who in turn smiled back. "I guess we should help as well," the druid offered. "Zek, Lent, and I would do this."

Zelner stood up from his chair both remembering when the druid had helped him personally so long ago. At that time, it hadn't been so bad, though four good elves had been killed and two heroic humans went into the Deep South to find an old sword that hasn't been discovered just yet.

CHAPTER SIX

As the sun rose from behind a far off mountain, Randle looked at the sight and listened to the sounds of the morning, knowing what may happen at Hell Mountain. *Will they get caught or will they be successful?* These were the thoughts that the druid had on his mind; he then glanced back at the two who were still asleep.

Funny, he thought. *I have no idea why the druid counsel has faith in Zek. He's a halfling of no importance.* Unless there's something that they are not telling me, what is it?

Then he glanced at Lent, *Taking Lent with me I can see. He's a born warrior and a damn good cook.* Then he set his eyes on the horizon yet again.

It's best we left the others now, he thought. *They would insist on coming.*

Hearing movement in the bushes not too far way, he had an idea of who it might be. Walking up to the thick green bushes, he parted them and saw Gandis and Talin. Randle shook his head. He knew their intention and he welcomed it. It was hard leaving behind friends, but they weren't making it any easier.

"What are you doing here?" he exclaimed.

Then some of the others came out. "Your friend told us

you'd be here." Gandis informed the druid.

Randle smiled at the thought and nodded.

"Where are the others?" Randle had to ask.

"With Darren's army," Talin told him, and the druid frowned, knowing his friend would put the rest of the group with Darren's army. Then he added, "I haven't seen Jack. Have you?"

Randle moved his eyes hoping that they would not notice, but he gave up the ruse before his friends started to question him. "I sent him on a few missions, which need to be done. Reid, my s- a good friend of mine" Randle said hoping that no one noticed the change of words. "Anyway this was only for the three of us," Randle said to him.

"Darren never told you that," said Talin. "He told you the three of you had a mission you had to do. Besides, he found out an elf was killed a few days ago."

Randle looked concerned at the news. He knew that Lent needed to know about the latest news.

"I already knew about that. My father told me," Lent said as he walked over to the group. "I also knew that he would send you here." Lent looked away feeling light-headed from getting up too fast.

"When did you talk to the king?" the druid wondered, not sure where this was going.

"I told you I had to pee," said Lent, "but I didn't. I rushed home, and he told me what had happened."

Randle looked surprised; he knew what it was like to lose a loved one.

"Look, Ra--" Lent began but stopped since he sensed trouble in the air.

"I sense trouble, too," the druid stated and ushered the others back into the bushes, but he stayed where he was. Then he moved forward to see what was coming. Peering from behind a tree, he gasped at what he saw: miles of trolls and gnomes and Orcs along with three other races of nameless creatures. He gasped again, stunned with disbelief, and also amazed by the size of Avlon's army. *Damn*, he thought.

Randle knew that the Avlon the shape shifter had further interests in dominating all of the land of Twilight.

"What the hell is that druid doing?" Gandis asked.

Zek began to speak, but realized he couldn't find the words. He now knew that he could leave since no one was paying any attention to him.

Have to get to Wellness, Zek thought and slipped out from behind a bush, silently the halfling walked away from the small group and moved toward the cursed village that lay in the distance. It is said that an evil wizard, Flander, put a curse on the place, but it didn't bother him. He knew it was on the way to Hell Mountain.

Wellness was founded over four hundred years ago, it is said that the town was built over a talisman of some sort. Some believed it a sword, others thought it a knife, but, in truth, no one really knew what it was or, for that matter, where it was buried. Only one man had seen it, but that was slightly over a century ago. He claimed that it wasn't a weapon at all, that it was a jewel.

Walking into the town, Conner the wizard smiled to himself as he looked over the townspeople. *I haven't been here for so long.* Then he shifted his eyesight so he could see better and spotted a halfling walking as fast he could go two miles away. *So Zek is returning.* He blinked, turning off the wizard sight. *The prophecy is happening.*

As dusk settled that evening, the little halfling reached

the cursed village. Two guards blocked the way, one tall and bearded, the other fat and short. Zek noticed the village wasn't much to look at; trees were everywhere, some near buildings, others were lined down the single circle. It only had a single store at the centre of the village. A sign read Dragon's Keeper. The building next door was just a house, but beside that was a strange looking building that Zek had never seen before. The roof was made out of some sort of metal, as the walls looked like wood but wasn't. It was some sort of brown marble.

"State your business," the tall bearded man said as he tried not to scratch his face, and the halfling looked up at him slightly perplexed.

"I'm here to see Fingers," Zek told them, and the guards glanced at each other. They knew the halfling but still they had a job to do. Zek moved forward but was stopped by the fat man that had a big nose, as he liked to drink. His lips were normal looking but his chin puffed out to make him look a bit like the over risen bread.

"Hold on a minute," the fat one said. He had on a soldier's uniform that was way too small for him. Stepping back a few steps, the two conversed, speaking in a whispered way so the halfling would not hear. Then the thin one left while the fat man moved forward.

"You letting me in, fatty?" the halfling said insolently, teasing his friend.

"I'm not fat," the guard snarled, not liking the joke one bit, and the halfling looked him up and down.

"Uniform too small for you, or can you tell me why your stomach is bigger than it used to be?" Zek stated with a smile.

The guard opened his eyes and arms wide.

"Zek!" he greeted him with a smile. "Sorry, old friend.

I don't see well at night. This isn't my uniform. I lost mine a week ago. As for my weight, I haven't been on active duty." He noticed the other guard come up.

"Fingers will see you now," the tall guard stated and showed him the way. Looking back, the halfling noticed a new guard take over the shift. "Who's that?" he asked.

The six foot guard looked at the halfling.

"That's my brother."

Zek looked pleased. "I thought so. He's built like you. Unlike Fatty." The guard one looked down again and noticed for the first time that it was his old friend.

"Zek." He beamed in delight.

Zek smiled back and Jerry stopped him.

"Before you go in, Fingers has been acting weird lately, issuing commands that don't make sense. Just be careful of what you say."

The halfling looked concerned.

"That I will. I'll see you around, Jerry." Zek said thinking the matter over as he strolled over to his friends cabin that lay off to his right. He knocked on the door a few seconds later., he heard a man inside say,

"Come in." The halfling entered and saw his old friend in the darkness. Something was definitely off about the man.

"Please come into the light," Fingers requested.

Zek, looking around the cabin, noticed a painting of the countryside that brightened the room, which seemed odd to the halfling, but the other walls were empty as if someone else lived there.

"What brings you here, Zek? I hope it's dangerous like the last adventure we had."

Zek thought a moment about the statement that Jerry had told him. Adventure and danger sprang into the halfling's mind.

"It sure was," Zek claimed and sat down on a pile of pillows. *This isn't my friend,* he thought. *Should I give him a pile of lies, which the imposter would swallow?*

"So, what can I do for you?" Fingers asked, and the halfling smiled brightly at him.

"I need you to find out the evil master's name," Zek said trying to trap who ever it was that looked like his friend. The imposter smiled weakly.

"His name is Avlon Klynn. As for where he came from, it's a mystery. No one really knows, though I could send someone to find out." Zek nodded in approval then added.

"I thank you for the name." *Avlon Klynn,* he thought then scratched his head. "Fingers," he said with a puzzled look on his face, "I want you to come with me to this land that he comes from."

The man started to laugh at the halfling's suggestion. Either he found it funny the way the halfling put it or the idea itself. However, it seemed to Zek that the man before him was now in a good mood.

"That would take a long time, old friend." Fingers glanced at one of the walls then back again. "As long as no druids come with us."

The halfling knew that part was true because he and Fingers had to deal with a druid once before and were burned badly. Since then, Fingers avoided magic users.

The imposter noted the false smile the halfling gave him.

"I'll come," he said and then changed his tone into a growl. "If by any chance any druids or mages come near me, I swear I'll kill them." Then he moved away sharply, breaking off the conversation. "OUT," he shouted and the halfling left in a hurry, thinking that he should tell someone of his encounter with the imposter.

Fingers paced the length of his hut, mad at himself for over-playing the part. *I have to kill that halfling and the others; they suspect that I'm not Fingers.* Then he slammed his hand down onto a table, which collapsed with the impact.

"If I ever see Avlon Klynn ever again, I'll kill him for putting me here." Opening his door to talk to Jerry, he said, "Tell Zek I'm sorry, but a few others will go in my place. It's time to reclaim what is ours." He closed his door, letting his guards know that he needed to be alone for some time. *I'll not only kill you, cousin Avlon. I'll kill off the rest of my race and declare myself ruler of this planet.*

Then he smirked to himself. *It would have been better if we had never come to this earth.* He then changed into a halfling. *I alone will breed all races out leaving only one race. If any of them truly knew what I intend to do,* he added and morphed back into Fingers. He chuckled as his eyes sparkled by the prospect of his little scheme.

CHAPTER SEVEN

As a foot landed on a pile of bones, they cracked under the pressure. "Careful," Bremin said to the human as he then bent down to study the remains.

"Are you fine, Bobby?" Bremin asked with clenched teeth since he had hurt his foot, but he ignored it for now, and Bobby slowly got up.

"What's going on up there?" a voice called out.

"Can any of you shut up?" snarled Bremin as he leaned on a cave wall. "Something isn't right." He thought a moment. *After Zek's disappearance, Avlon's army advanced toward the group as if Zek were keeping them at bay. But that wasn't so; the army had been forcing the group into the tunnels of the dead.*

However, both Randle and Bremin had been in the tunnels before, some leading into Hell Mountain itself. Others branched off into the grey world where dangerous beasts lay in wait to pounce on their prey, and it unhinged the group.

"This way," Bremin told the others frightened that something would go wrong.

Randle smiled as Bremin pointed to the tunnel to indicate where to go. *Good*, he thought. *He knows the tunnels as I do.* He followed the rest.

Whatever are you doing, Zek, I sure hope you aren't fooled by Fingers. The last I heard, he was killed by a Tekker. He shook his head trying to get rid of the thought. *However, if he finds out the shape shifter took up the guise of the human...* He stopped in his tracks. *Zek's in trouble. If he finds out that Fingers is someone else, he could be killed.*

Then he moved back to the entrance, which was only ten feet away. Waiting out the enemy as the army pressed on, he stayed in the shadows of the cave to stay hidden from sight. He thought as he stood there, *what of the others? They can look after themselves.*

Standing in the dark, he remembered the green, blue, and red elf stones that they found. As Randle reached into his pocket, he felt around for them.

"Gone," he whispered. "Zek's more resourceful than I thought."

Then he remembered that, whoever had the stones, they would protect him. *I'll go just in case the Tekker tries to harm him.* Then he saw the last of trolls move beyond the hills.

Once in the night air, the druid moved his hands over his own body slowly at first but he moved them faster and faster gathering up the magic to transport himself. Light gathered around him until he disappeared from sight.

Boy, thought Zek, *tomorrow we leave for the land of Charnic.* He saw someone appear in front of him, where he was housed for the night.

"Randle!" Zek said in surprise but was glad to see the druid. "You can't stay," Zek blurted out.

"I know, Zek. Before I go, I have to tell you that Fingers is no longer. He has been replaced by a Tekker."

He noticed that the halfling didn't flinch in surprise. "You know."

"I do. I've been playing a game with the Tekker. That's why I took the stones." He showed them to Randle, and then placed them back in the pouch. The druid was surprised, and the small man nodded, "I've known for some time." He added, "Avlon came from Charnic."

The druid now remembered. "He built an army there," the druid recalled, "but he was betrayed by a shape shifter." In all the lands, every druid had to talk to each other since it helped not to forget. Even if they didn't know, the council would be able to get to the ancient books of the old world. The higher counsel knew that the Tekkers were alien to the planet, but they kept the secret to themselves. In orbit, the rest of humanity flew in space ships fighting the enemy at all costs, but the colonies were losing the battle. Randle remembered something mentioned in one of the books, staring at the halfling what seemed like a lifetime.

The little man looked concerned for his friend and asked,

"Is something wrong, Randle?"

"I've got to go." Randle then added, "Be careful, young one," and the druid vanished a second later.

"Open up," a guard shouted, and Zek went to unlock the door. The door was pushed opened, which caused him to fall and the elf stones fell to the ground. Fingers stared at the little man.

"I sensed magic in here," he said coldly and then noticed the elf stones lying on the floor. "What's this?" he asked. He bent down, took the stones in his hands, and got back up.

"Sir," the two guards said, stunned by the man's appearance.

"What is it, fools?"

Zek backed against the wall, trying to stay way from the Tekker at all costs. Rushing into the room, the guards took in the scene and noticed the Tekker. Zek ran out of the hut and went over to the barracks. He knocked on the door, but no one answered.

"Jerry, what's going on?" Fingers asked in puzzlement, not knowing what was going on but then noticed that his men surrounded him. "Jerry, Doyle, what's going on?" he asked, concerned about his situation.

"Where is he?" Jerry growled in anger as he lifted his sword. The Tekker had no idea of what was happening. "TELL ME!" Jerry snapped angrily, but still the Tekker had no idea. He glanced at the wall and noticed that the wall was covered with mirrors.

The door to the barracks finally opened.

"Help!" the halfling cried in despair waking up the rest of the village. "Jerry and Doyle are in trouble." Five soldiers picked up their weapons. Rushing over to the hut, the five noticed the Tekker for the first time. They were armed, as were Jerry and Doyle. The Tekker dropped the stones as he noticed the halfling, and his mask went back up.

"We suspected that you were a Tekker," Jerry told him. "Now tell us, where the hell is Fingers?" he said coldly hoping to get an answer.

"I'll tell you before I die," the Tekker said, defeated. "He's in the grey world, serving a beast."

Jerry looked pleased, as did the others. "Kill him," Jerry ordered his men. He knew the order had to be given, and this imposter had to die. His troops chopped and plunged their weapons into the Tekker until he died.

Picking up the elf stones from the floor, Zek glanced

over at Jerry and the others shouted with glee since they
had been freed from their fake leader. Jerry clasped his
hands on the halfling and lifted him in the air. "To
Freedom!" he shouted. "To our new leader!"

Zek looked stunned by the news. He looked at the
troops and smiled in utter victory.

"We will rescue you brother." Jerry stated. Then he
choked a second when everyone started to bring out the
beer. A single tear ran down his cheek, saddened by his loss
and his gain. He now knew that his brother was alive and
well.

As the group followed the tunnel, Bremin looked
puzzled. "This is not supposed to bend here." Lent looked
at the wall, which was bending in the wrong direction.

"Maybe things have changed," one of the others said.

Bremin nodded. "You might be right about that. It has
been a long time since I came down here." Then he walked
further on, not noticing the trap up ahead.

"You okay, Tunalun?" Bremin shouted back since he
was also looking ahead. He looked at Talin for a moment,
sensing that something wasn't right, but he shook it off as if
it were nothing.

"Fine, it's…" and he felt tiny neck hairs stick up in
fright, and he noticed a shadow move.

"Fall back!" Bremin shouted warning the others as
Tunalun grabbed his sword and started to slice at the
shadows.

"No spider traps me," Tunalun whispered harshly, he
felt his blood pump and his heart begin to race, "and gets
away with it."

The others now knew what the monsters where. "Stick
with me," Bremin urged the group, but he watched Tunalun

as he battled the spiders. With sword in hand, Tunalun swiped at the spiders. He uttered a magic word, which sent his sword aflame, which lit up the area. He made the spiders back up a bit, but not by much. A spider came forward only to have its leg taken off.

"They've trapped us," Lent called out. "The escape route is blocked by these things."

"Get near me," Bremin urged them, but the spiders tried to separate them. "Tun, Lent, I want you both to take the back end, and the rest of us will attack the front." Bremin shouted commands at every single member. A spider jumped at Lent only to be impaled by a sword. Another attacked over the corpse of the dead spider only to receive a blow to the head, the sword cutting into it as its blood oozed out.

Lent now noticed that he was no longer in the party, but was surrounded by the spiders. "HELP!" he screamed as a spider knocked him to the ground. He stabbed it in the eye, which made the spider mad. Another leg pinned his hand to the ground, so the elf could not do anything, "BREMIN!" he yelled with all his might, frightened and alone.

Bremin heard the scream, as did the others. The spiders had separated them. "I'M COMING!" Bremin shouted back and sliced a spider in two. Two spiders jumped at him, one on the right, and the other on the left. He rolled out of their way just in time as he ran toward his friend.

"I'M COMING!" he shouted again and faced a giant female spider bigger than the rest. His face went ash white from the encounter. He swiped with his sword, which sliced off a leg. The mother spider screamed in pain, but lunged at the elf hoping to kill him. Bremin hit the spider again, but this time the sword hit it in the head and was buried. The body of the spider fell lifeless; it turned over onto its back as the legs folded up., He looked over to see Lent busy with his free hand, trying to keep the spiders off him since a he was pinned to the ground.

"I've got to go," Bremin told the dead mother spider and pulled out the sword that was dripping wet with spider blood. Then he quietly impaled another spider as it advanced on him from behind, only killing it in one strike.

Leaping over the monster spider, he landed onto the back of the spider that had pinned Lent to the ground, which killed it. "Thanks a bunch," his friend said and sprang to his feet as it rolled up like the mother spider. Another spider burst into flames a second later.

Bremin noticed the newcomer flaming up the spiders. "WHO ARE YOU?" he shouted over the roar of the spiders.

"Who I am is of no importance. I'm here to help." The newcomer smashed an axe into another spider as it shot webbing at an elf.

"Fall back," Bremin commanded his men, but the spiders were too near to do anything. "I've got to help them," he told the newcomer, thoughts of losing his friends like this was too painful to him he praying for the onslaught to end.

"As you command, elf," the stranger said, pleased to help someone for a change. He whispered something and every spider froze. "Hurry, it won't last long," the man told them, and the elves moved fast toward him. "Down this tunnel," the hermit said and the whole group followed, trying to keep up with the human.

Lent whispered in Bremin's ear.

"Can we trust him?"

Bremin looked forward, trying to make sure that the

human was ahead and out of hearing distance. "Not for a second. I think he planned the trap."

"Where are we going?" Bremin asked to the newcomer, trying to sound pleasant about it. Then he noticed the walls were alight. He couldn't tell where the light was coming from, Bremin looked everywhere, but still the source of the light could not be seen. He could tell something wasn't right about the man or the situation.

"Where are you taking us?" Bremin demanded, this time trying to get some answers, now showing his discomfort for once.

"Somewhere safe," came the man's reply, neither menacing nor friendly. He stepped away from the group; the elves heard a noise. They looked around trying to locate the sound. Suddenly, it sounded like iron gears. The group looked up just in time as a cage came down hard, which trapped them on the spot.

"Who are you?" Bremin demanded, but the man before them only smiled. "Why have you done this to us? We don't pose a threat to you," Bremin declared, angry at the situation.

The newcomer smiled madly at them as he lifted his arms into the air.

"To keep you here. I have been missing my race and the others. A tekker lured me into these caves long ago. At first, I thought it was my sister. I miss her so. It turned out it was a Tekker." He spat at the word and then looked at the group closely trying to see his old friend, but the halfling wasn't there.

"Do any of you know of Zek, the small halfling?"

Bremin stared at him trying to find out the man's angle in all of this as he nodded.

"We all do. Why you ask?" Bremin replied, studied

him. He needed to know who this man was , and who had planned this but his questions will be answered in time.

"You see this book?" the hermit said as he picked up a red book and showed it to them. "It's said in it that a halfling will restore the lands." Then he looked down at the dirt. "Sad really. It also says that the halfling would free an old friend." Then he walked away from the group muttering to himself.

Bremin just couldn't understand why they had been taken prisoner. He mulled it over in his head. The man was alone; he could see it as well as the others of this small group. What was his connection to Zek? The book was another question, which slightly puzzled him.

Pacing back and forth in a chamber that had paintings of old druids and a few chairs scattered about, the druid called Palmer listened to the story that his old friend was telling him. Palmer had closed cropped, brown hair and wore a green robe that hung to the soles of his feet.

"Anyway, may I have the book I need?" Randle asked, happy to see his stepbrother, who he hadn't seen in four months. His smile gave him away. The druid in front of him smiled weakly as he raised his arms in defense.

"Don't ask me. Books are usually kept in the library," came the reply. The two had a quick hug. The brothers were glad to see each other.

"I'm talking about the book of prophecies," Randle said as he smiled at his stepbrother once again as he noted the discomfort that Palmer had.

"It's gone," his stepbrother told him.

"Gone? When will it be back?"

Palmer looked agitated as if something had happened not to long ago.

"It was stolen, was it?" Randle exclaimed since he noticed the unease of his stepbrother. Palmer nodded.

"A warlock stole the book. I can't really tell you very much. By the time we realized we had an intruder, the book was gone. But he did leave this." He showed Randle a symbol of a great fox under it a single word Eternity, which meant something to Randle.

"Morranden," he breathed as he narrowed his eyes, Randle was not happy to see the symbol since he knew the man was still married to his ex-wife. *You always thought you were the best witch around Trish. Morrandon must have been hired to steal the book.* Then he studied the symbol more carefully.

Hold on. What's this? Randle thought, noticing that the symbol was the one that he gave Trish long ago since he had his name of the back. *Bad, he's playing with fire.* Randle looked up at Palmer.

"I'll find this thief," Randle promised , displeased with his brother in law.

"You know this thief, don't you?" Palmer said.

Randle nodded.

"He's Trish's husband."

Palmer placed a hand on the druid's shoulder.

"Careful, I hear this person can kill anyone that comes in contact with him," but Randle knew how to handle himself around the man.

"There's something I haven't told you." Randle declared.

Palmer stood, willing to listen to the tale.

"When I was working with Avlon, I met the man. Morranden is pure evil. That's why he married my ex; he did it to impress his boss and to stomp on my dreams."

Palmer shook his head at the news.

"I had no idea. As far as you working for Avlon, we all knew about that. You may have done many horrible things in your past, but we are only looking forward. We trust you, and I hope you can find this warlock."

Randle stepped away from his stepbrother. He dared not to cry in front of him; he was too proud for that. He needed to be alone for a little more time to figure out his next move.

Entering the aptly named village of Small, the companions looked around at the ten houses that are all laced with twine as a single pub sat in the middle of the village. It was within a wood, which made it look beautiful. Flowers scattered the area, making it look peaceful.

As Jandis stepped up to the inn, he noticed that the sign was crooked; it said Dragons Born Inn and Pub. Shannon glanced at the dwarf, making sure to keep his eye on him. He didn't trust the dwarf at all; well, he didn't trust anyone, not even the elf that stood by him.

"What are you thinking, Shannon?" Ricla asked as she placed her hand on his shoulder.

"Don't touch me," he growled at her and looked at Jack for a brief second. "Your army will be lead here, to stay the night. Just don't get any ideas to mess this up. I plan on delivering the dwarf to Avlon." He realized he had told them too much. "Inside," he ordered sharply.

The four entered the inn. It wasn't classy, but it would do for the four of them. They looked at the walls, which were covered with pictures of Dragons fighting Orcs and gnomes. In another picture, Shannon noticed a dragon fighting what looked a half horse, half man.

They all glanced at each other; walls were packed with the pictures. It unnerved Shannon to see so many pictures of Dragons. He had heard tales of the creatures, but seeing this much attention to these creatures just made him uneasy.

"I'll be right back," Ricla told the men and left the inn a moment later.

Upon leaving the building, the young elven girl walked through the village. Jack had gotten to the village an hour before the small group. He followed her. As he hid behind bushes, a few people saw her as she neared a bush that lay beyond the inn. The elven Princess noticed it catch on fire. The flames were bluish so it would not burn the bush, and then a face appeared.

"Did they fall for it, my lovely?" Avlon asked with a slight grin.

"They sure did. We're in Small at the moment. They don't suspect a thing. Send the army right away," Ricla told her boss as he smiled back toward her.

The face disappeared after a few seconds. Jack had seen the scene then went back to the village of where he came from, and then thought better for it since he had to report his findings.

Turning around, Jack made a beeline for the elven army to inform them that Avlon would be sending an army to Small since Ricla had told her boss about the location. He had gone his own way to find out all about the Princess and why she was betraying her people to the evil master. Now he knew what the Princess was planning and why, but he could not accept the fact that she was brainwashed by the Tekker. He turned away from the village.

Jack thought about his master as well. Was I brainwashed? Jack thought. Brail would not brainwash others to join his cause; he would only convert them.

As he walked down the path, Jack noticed it was

slowly getting dark. He heard birds overhead and other animals around him. He noted a chipmunk that looked up at him then scurry off, as if Jack was unimportant in some way.

"Pssst," Jack heard from behind a tree to his right, so he stepped over slightly, trying not to make a sound.

"What did you find out?" Darren asked, still hiding behind the tree as Jack pretended to relieve himself.

"Ricla is in Small with Jandis and the others. You were right about her. She has changed. At least we got here first. Your contact was right. There is going to be an attack." He paused for a second, knowing that Darren was pleased since all was going well. "Though we might have a problem, a man has turned up. A human."

"He could be willing to free the others," Darren suggested.

"Not what I saw. I know his ambitions, sir"

"How's that?"

"He's a dwarf hunter, sir. They usually care for one thing, to get their prize and leave. My guess is he intends to take the dwarf back to Avlon."

Darren took in the news of the dwarf hunter.

"Any more news about him, Jack?"

"Yes, I saw him four years ago while I was traveling with friends. I learned his name."

"Which is?" Darren wondered slightly.

"His name is Shannon Lee."

The leader looked startled by the name. *It can't be,* Darren thought. He had heard stories about the man; some said that he took on a hundred men and killed every single one. Another said he had helped a local vampire to get rid of a great threat of unspeakable evil. Then he reached out his hand, only revealing his arm from his hiding place.

"Here," Darren said, holding a big bag of gold.

Jack peered inside the bag and smiled.

"Randle will be pleased," the spy told Darren. He began to move off .not wishing to give the bag to Randle at all. Jack had other ideas for the gold, and none of them was legal.

"Ricla, where did you go? For a moment there, I thought you left us," Reid asked the elf as she sat down on a chair beside him.

"Nature calls us all," she remarked sarcastically and smiled slightly. Then she noticed Jandis walked up to them.

"Where's Shannon Lee?" Jandis asked kindly, making sure all was fine.

"The last time I saw him he was at the bar," Reid said as he pointed toward the bar.

Jandis walked up to the bar with an eager smile.

"What will it be?" asked the bearded tavern keep as he handed over a glass of ale to a customer.

"Your finest ale," he beamed. "Have you seen a tall man with a knife as a side arm?"

The owner nodded as he poured the ale into a glass.

"Out back, talking to someone," the man replied as he handed over the ale.

The dwarf gave the man two gold coins.

"Thanks," Jandis said as he took a sip, liking the ale greatly. In one gulp, the ale disappeared. Jandis handed the glass back, and he headed to the back door only to hear voices.

"I tell you, Larry, this is going my way. All I have to do is to kill the human and the elf and sell the dwarf to Avlon Klynn. I will be rich again," Shannon said as he patted the man's shoulder. Shannon heard footsteps in the distance. He tried to see where they were coming from, but the dwarf could see a lot better at night than any human. Beyond Shannon, he could see trolls of every size and gnomes along with other races.

"Oh, no," Shannon whispered to his friend as he covered his eyes with his left hand. He noticed arrows raining down from the trees, killing the first wave of the intruders. The dwarf bolted out of the door, which startled the two men, and shouted, "GET INSIDE, NOW!"

The villagers scrambled for their homes, not ready for the attack. Some tripped over roots only to meet mud since it was raining. None were harmed yet, but the villagers were frightened. Thousands of their enemy advanced on them, some dying in traps that the elves had built, but the enemy marched on, determined to kill any that got in their way.

"ATTACK!" Darren shouted in fury and lifted up his sharp sword. He smacked a gnome on its head, which killed it instantly. He turned fast to his right, swung his blade into a troll's stomach, and tore it open, spilling its intestines. He pulled it free and smiled.

"The battle for freedom begins!" Darren shouted since he was excited to see some action for once. Killing an enemy while it was asleep was not his idea of honor, but killing in a battle was very different; it meant true honor. .

Hour after hour it lasted. Neither Darren nor the others noticed the time, but finally he felt tired and noticed that Avlon's great army wasn't able to thin down his ranks. Arrows flew into the air and killed several of the enemy. By morning, both armies were too tired to continue. The small group of elves and humans were neither wounded nor killed. For the great army of Avlon, a thousand troops were killed, who were left on the field by their comrades in arms.

"Shannon, wake up," Jandis urged the human while holding his throat.

Shannon opened his eyes; he felt the hands on his throat. He seized his knife that lay that beside him. Shannon moved his arm fast enough to place the blade under the dwarf's neck.

"You murderous dwarf," Shannon growled and kept his knife at the dwarf's throat. Jandis did not dare move. This took him by surprise, and he feared for his life. "Take your hands off me," Shannon commanded. Then he noticed that the dwarf looked frightened and was removing his hands slowly.

"I'd rather be dead than be Avlon's slave," Jandis spat, now no longer afraid as Shannon put his knife away, tucking it out of sight.

"I suspected you heard my conversation when I noticed you bolt outside. If it weren't for you, I would have to fight." Shannon got up off the bed and straightened his clothes. "Besides, my plans have changed for now, dwarf." He pulled the bedclothes off the bed. "Right now I can't get the things I want."

The dwarf looked puzzled at first. "Sounds to me you have given up on hunting my race."

"I have," Shannon told him, feeling disappointed in himself for not leaving before the attack.

"Don't fool yourself. You'll always be a hunter of some sort." Jandis noticed the human smiling.

"You just renewed my faith, dwarf," Shannon said as he patted the dwarf on the shoulder,

"Great," said Jandis. "I can't believe I opened my big mouth."

Shannon looked down at his prize. "Relax, after this attack is over, I'll be taking you. This setback will only take a week." *I have faith that Avlon will win this battle*, he thought.

Joining the others a few seconds later, Shannon had the feeling that the group was pinned down. Shaking off the bad feeling and the thought, he noticed that the leader of the human resistance was waving them over. Ricla walked up to Shannon and yawned since she was still groggy from sleep.

"Over here," Darren called out, and the four rushed over to see what the man wanted. Eyeing the new member with interest, Darren related the news of the attack.

"I can't believe this is happening," Ricla said, showing concern for the men that surrounded her, but it was only a show.

What a piece of work, Shannon thought. "I'm..." he began. Then a vision sprang into his mind. People of all sizes lay dead in the village. The vision focused onto a troll as a father tried to protect his child.

"Please, don't kill me," he pleaded. *"I'll be Avlon's slave,"* he cried as he kept the child close to him.

The troll smiled wickedly at the thought. "No, we'll take the child, not you." It chopped off the man's head. The boy screamed in shock and fear as the troll hovered over the boy.

"You are now Avlon's son."

Shaking the vision away a second later, Shannon noticed that the others were watching him.

"Are you all right?" Darren asked, concerned for the young man. "We'd better get going if we're off to Hell Mountain."

Shannon placed his hand on the man's shoulder. "You

can't leave," Shannon stated, and the leader looked puzzled.

"We just rescued Small from an attack."

"Yeh, one of many."

"How do you know that? Do you belong to Avlon?"

"No… I can't explain it … its just I… get these visions at certain times, and they're always right. The last time I had one was seventeen years ago," he lied. "It showed my parents were killed by Orcs. At first, I thought it was a dream. When I got back to Canor, I found the town destroyed," Shannon lied again, but some of it was true. He had averted the crisis and changed his parent's lives for the better. He turned away to hide his pain, and the tears that ran down his cheeks. He had kept his feelings bottled up for too long. The massive group behind him looked surprised by the news.

"It must have been horrible for you," Ricla admitted.

He turned toward her and his mood changed. He snarled at her, "You may act concerned, Ricla, but you can't fool me. You betrayed your people when Avlon took you." Then he paused for a moment, not willing to expose himself any more than was necessary. "She wasn't brainwashed, you fools. She gave him the secrets willingly."

The others looked surprised.

"How do you know?" Jack asked.

"I was there when it happened," Shannon replied with was a lie in it self..

"Okay," Darren said, somewhat believing the boy as two of his guards took her prisoner. "Now do you have proof of this vision of yours?" he asked.

Shannon nodded. "I do. If you please follow me, I'll show you." He showed Darren the way to the hill. Shannon wasn't taking any mistakes in his judgment. He made sure none of the sentries saw them, and he poked his head out slightly. "There's your proof," he whispered harshly.

Darren opened his mouth, stunned by the sight. It looked as if they were getting ready for a war. He followed the outline of the army; it just didn't seem to end. Within the army of Avlon's forces, a war banner could be seen. Darren looked the other way; still he could not see the end. There were more Orcs and trolls than he had ever seen in his short life all banded together for a common cause. He heard a trumpet ahead of him, another sounded off to his right, then to his left. More could be heard all about them, they were surrounded.

"Dear Zantra," Darren whispered in horror, he had a sinking feeling that his own army would lose this battle.

Not liking the name, the two crawled back to the others, undetected.

"Something wrong, Boss?" asked one of the soldiers as Darren and Shannon walked up to them, horror still plastered on Darren's face.

"Get back to your posts. There's an army out there that will not give up." Seeing his right-hand man running up, Darren stopped himself a few feet away. "Report, soldier."

The man breathed in a few breaths. "We're surrounded sir. There is no way around," he informed his commander.

"I know. I heard the trumpets, too," Darren said but did not show his fear.

Jandis smiled at his captor. "Looks like we're going to be here for more than a week."

Shannon glanced at him with narrow eyes, wishing that they hadn't stayed the night at all.

"You just wait little man; I will do my duty to keep you alive." He moved toward the inn, not willing to hear what the others had to say.

CHAPTER EIGHT

As Bremin lay on the hard, stony ground, he watched his friends sleep. *We have to find a way out,* he thought. Slowly he got up after a stone hit him on his shoulder. Looking down at the small rock, he bent over to study it. It looked slightly different to him. As he looked above him he smiled as he noticed a small hole above them which was slightly bigger than the size of a man.

Our way out, he thought. *Thank God, there's a hole.* Seeing the blue sky through it, he knew they were rescued. Finding handholds, he started to climb. After several minutes, which seemed like a lifetime, he reached the top and pulled himself out only to be blinded by sunlight.

"Bremin," a soft voice said, and he turned away from the sun to see a halfling. His vision cleared to show the halfling smiling back to him. Once out of the hole, Bremin looked around him, amazed that an army had made camp just above them.

"Who's the one that dropped a rock through the hole?" Bremin said as he rubbed his shoulder.

"I did," Zek said feeling slightly guilty for what he did. "I didn't know you were down there."

"It's good to see you, Zek. I have to get the others out. As for the small rock, I'll survive," Bremin told the group as he realized that the great human army that surrounded him. "I know this area!" Bremin said suddenly and shook his head. "We've traveled in a circle!" He did not believe his luck. "Soldier, what's your name?"

"James, sir. Zek is our leader for now." The soldier looked down at the halfling. "He commanded us to find you at all costs." James added, "If it weren't for the elf stones, we would not have found you. It's lucky you came up when you did. We were about to leave." Then he looked down into the hole.

"Morgan, bring the rope," Jerry commanded a young man, and the teen rushed over with the rope in hand. A rope was lowered into the hole and tied to a nearby tree. Bremin climbed back down the rope and shook his friends awake. "Talin, we're rescued," he said with a smile.

"I knew Randle would," he said.

"Wasn't the druid, Talin. It's Zek."

Talin looked surprised at the news still it was good to be rescued, Talin thought.

"No one's going anywhere," snarled their captor, as the human pushed a hidden button that lay hidden on the cavern wall. The cave roof collapsed as people jumped out of the way of the falling rocks and earth, which filled the air with dust. Some of the army fell into the small cavern, but not too many, less than a handful. People coughed as the dust settled. At least no one was hurt from the impact.

"You'll never escape me ever again," the hermit laughed evilly.

Looking at the hermit, Jerry stared, studying the bearded man from behind the bars that separated them.

"Fingers?" Jerry whispered in surprise, not believing his luck at seeing his own brother once again. The hermit raised his eyes at the name. He walked over to the familiar man.

"Who are you? And how do you know my name?" Fingers replied coldly, since he had no idea who the man was, yet he seemed familiar to him.

The army of humans reached out to touch their lost leader. As the rest of the army from above stared down in disbelief, they called out, "It's us, Fingers."

A tear rolled down Jerry's cheek. Happy to see his brother once again, a smile formed on his face.

"Don't you remember me, brother?" Jerry said as Fingers stood there shocked by the news.

Jerry, Jerry, raced through the man's mind. *I know that name but where...* It dawned on him.

"Brother," he whispered in delight. A tear ran down his cheek as he released the latch for the cell, and it disappeared into the wall.

The two men walked toward each other. "I missed you," both said at the same time and gave each other a warm hug. It had been along time since they last saw each other.

"I thought I'll never see you ever again," Fingers told him. Then he related the tale of how the Tekker tricked him into the caves.

"Amazing," Jerry said. "For a long time, I thought you were dead, but we found out not too long ago otherwise. The Tekker told us before he died."

"Did he die horribly?" the hermit asked as he smiled happily. He looked back at his home, which he had for the past year or two. "Hand me a blade," he suggested to his brother.

Handing over his blade over, Jerry then followed the hermit to a small lake.

"He sure looks different," a soldier said. "It's as

though he's a different man."

Watching the two leave, Bremin turned to look at the commander in charge.

"What are you thinking?" Bremin asked in wonderment.

"I'm thinking he can no longer be free. Besides, being alone for a long time can change any man. Though it's really up to Jerry to make the decision not me." The soldier said as he turned away and barked an order, "Get us out of this hole."

"Who's that?" Talin asked seeing a form being lowered into the cavern.

"You'll find out," the commander said, and a small hooded man came up.

"Zek," Talin whispered. "So…it is true."

Bremin overheard his fellow elves.

"Zek," Bremin said aloud, and the others heard the name. Bremin smiled weakly. "I saw him up top," he told his comrades. They just stood there dumbfounded.

"It's me," Zek agreed and smiled at the group. "Sorry for leaving, but I had other things to do now that I'm back before we go to Small to lend a hand in the fighting"

"Fighting?" the elves said surprised at the word.

"Yes, fighting. Our forces have been gathering there, and they are under attack by Avlon's army," the halfling told the elves.

"For what purpose?" Bremin wondered. Then he realized something bad might have happened at the village.

"How many troops do you have…because, I would help out."

The commander smiled at the thought. "No need, elf. Zek has other plans for you. He'll inform you about your dangerous mission."

As Zek told Bremin and Talin what their mission was, the two agreed since it would take them along time to get to East Side Edge, which was far away. It would take them at least four good years to travel, since there weren't any gates along the way. Both didn't say when they were going, but they both knew it was just as important to destroy Hell Mountain.

Randle had traveled a few miles to find new comrades to join him to free the centaurs and bring them back to Twilight at all costs .It was nearing night, and he spotted a camp fire up ahead, within the forest that lay before him .By the time it was dark, he was all most there.

Slowly, making sure that none of them heard him, his night shadow was the only thing that disturbed the night. The only person in the camp looked around him. He was spooked to the extreme since he wasn't sure what was going on.

"Ssssh," the wind sounded in his ear, and he jumped a little as a twig snapped in the forest, which caused the man to look in the direction of the sound, and he noticed the lone wolf running toward him. It's face was in a snarl, Anker jumped back a bit frightened by the approach of the animal.

At this point, the druid could see the man was terrified.

"BEGONE," the druid bellowed at the beast, and the giant wolf turned to leave, then thought differently and sat down on the spot.

"Go away," Randle told the beast with a stern look, but the man by the fire did not know what to do. As Randle lifted his arm, he summoned a ball of flame, which rushed at the imaginary animal. The ball of fire hit the animal in the rear making it yelp in fear. The ball of flame disappeared as if it wasn't there in the first place. Sitting down beside the human, Randle turned his head to look at him

"You okay?" Randle asked as the skinny man just smiled weakly, unsure of what to do.

"I," Anker began then rephrased his words, "thank you." He stared at the druid thankful the druid had shown up when he did, and then concentrated on getting back his nerve. "If you hadn't shown up, that beast would have killed me."

The druid knew the truth; he didn't tell the man that the wolf was an old trick to frighten people like him. That was the only trick the druid wanted to do.

"I need your help," the druid began as he warmed his hands by the fire.

"With what, Druid?" the man said angrily, then realized he was out of line.

"I'm looking for a great thief." Randle stated as Anker stared at him. What was going on? It sounded exciting so far; Anker was ready to take on any old adventure.

The shaggy haired man smiled as he gave the druid a stern look, unsure of trusting a druid at all. *A thief, no doubt,* the man thought. *Why would a druid want a thief... unless,* and then he looked back.

"I could help you, for a price," Anker told the druid.

"How's fifty gold pieces?" the druid offered.

The hunter smiled evilly, wanting to know where the gold was hidden.

"First of all you need to find the thief," Randle said playing with the human. He dared not smile nor laugh since he needed the hunter.

"Then I get the gold." Anker wondered.

"I will question the man or torture him if need be."

"That's when I get the gold."

The druid was planning mind games with the man, but he had no gold on hand .Randle was trying to see if he could trust the man with his life, since this was all a test.

"When he tells me want I'm looking for, then you get your gold," the druid told the man sternly.

"Whatever you say, druid." Pleased by the conversation, he held his water bottle in his hands and drank from it.

After a few minutes, Randle reached into his pocket and brought out a small, gold locket

"Well, you do have some use," the hunter stated, seeing the gold glisten in the night.

"First of all, what is your name, stranger?" The druid smiled at his own game.

"Anker," the hunter just said, staying calm though he did not like to be questioned in any manner. He realized that the druid was playing a dangerous game with him.

"Calm down, will you?" Randle told him and then lay on the ground a few feet from the fire to keep warm. Glancing over at the druid, Anker waited for a few minutes for the druid to fall asleep. Slowly going over to him as the druid rested, the hunter reached out to search the man's robes and found the locket, smiling to himself. He was pleased at the outcome. Getting back to his spot, he began to think. *That was too easy. What if the druid let me have it?* Then he shook his head, trying to forget about it.

Anker didn't realize that the druid's body wasn't by the fire any longer.

"I'll take that," the druid said and grabbed the locket from the man.

"How?" the hunter exclaimed then glanced over to the fake body. "Sneaky, aren't you?" he muttered harshly and then laughed in spite of himself.

"Take me to your friend, Anker," the druid said. "I know he stole the book." Then he grinned nastily at the hunter. "Don't ever do that again." Arcan moved away from the camp.

As night wore on, the two lay sleeping, but something woke the young druid. Lying still and pretending to sleep, he watched the as two humans that were trying to steal from them. He placed his hand in his pocket and discovered that the locket was still there. He put his other hand in the other pocket as if he were asleep; he turned a bit which startled the two that were fumbling about in the camp.

He threw a bottle into the bush, and it exploded on impact, causing the two to look up. Confusion filled their faces. A single form could be seen, but the smoke covered his face and his body.

"Who are you?" the druid demanded.

The two glanced at each other. Both stumbled. One fell to the ground; the other just wet his pants.

"WHO ARE YOU?" it yelled in fury.

"I'm Dexter, sir," said the five foot nine man that had wet his pants which embarrassed him.

"Why are you stealing this man's belongings? If you're planning to resell it, don't bother," the form told him, and the two swallowed, surprised that the centaur was ugly and nasty. Being a horse race, most of them are nice, but there were some that were as nasty as trolls or gnomes. Neither could be trusted, but no one had seen a centaur in over five hundred years, since the war started, that was when they disappeared.

Now Randle intended to bring them back at any cost since he alone knew where they were. Getting there was another thing since no mortal ever traveled that far, besides it was further than the gates could reach.

"Who are you?" Arcan commanded again, still on the ground, and the two looked over at him. They noticed that the creature was only an image.

"You have nerve, druid," Dexter said pleased to see his own father as he watched Randle get up from the ground. Open-mouthed, the man began to smile since he had met the druid so long ago. "It's good to see you again, Da... Randle," Dexter exclaimed then noticed the robe of the druid. "Not working for Avlon, I see," he wondered.

"Back to your old tricks, I see," Randle said, unsure if he should trust his own son now. "Stealing is not a good trade," Randle pointed out as Dexter emptied his pockets.

"Nor, is siding with the enemy," Dex pointed back. "I've got to get money somehow. Besides, I heard you've been flagging Avlon off lately. Not wise. I would rather be out of the way of the Tekker."

Randle noticed the hunter was stirring from his sleep.

"Help me, Dexter," Randle requested as he smiled as the two men stepped away to converse.

He turned back for a minute and listened further to what the druid intended to do. Dexter nodded.

"I'll help. Besides, the people of Hamlock are looking for me," Dexter said as he glanced over at his friend. "Dale, will help as well," but his friend didn't look pleased at the thought of it.

"I won't..." Dale began, but was cut off by his friend.

"You'll help," Dex snapped at him, "or I'll drag you to the dead forest."

The shoulder length dark haired man looked frightened by the threat; Dale knew that Dexter meant it since their last employer had lost his head. "Don't mind him, Randle.

He has no idea what Avlon is about.... Besides, I was hoping you'd get me to help." He smiled evilly for no reason. "Sometimes it's good to upset Avlon. He usually kills his followers and troops." Then he laughed at the thought. "So, what's first?" he asked.

"The book of prophecy and the thief. Unless you know who the thief is." It was Randle's turn to smile.

"Let me see, it's your ex-wife's husband," Dexter said as he grinned at his father, then noticed the sun was coming up as it crested a nearby mountain.

"I'm up," Anker said as he straightened his clothes as Randle looked over at the hunter

"I thought you were asleep!" Randle exclaimed.

The hunter smiled as he collected his things.

"How can I? With the two of you talking," the hunter snapped as he lifted the single bag over his shoulder and stepped forward. "Well?" the hunter said eagerly at the three of them. "You coming or what?"

The druid had a suspicion that the man was up to something.

CHAPTER NINE

Fingers waited until the water was still so he could see him self and then started to cut at the long hairs of his beard with the borrowed knife until his chin became visible for the first time in ages. This was his first time cutting off the beard since he didn't have a knife before.

"They're not your friends," his image said to him, but he ignored the comment. "Friends don't force you to leave," it said, but Fingers was desperately trying not to hear. "They don't deserve you," it mocked him. Fingers dropped the knife and splashed his hand down into the water since he was up set with the water demon.

"SHUT UP," Fingers hissed in a whisper.

"No, I won't. Nor shall I let them take you."

"Don't ever," Fingers warned as he gritted his teeth. His anger got the better of him. "Defy me." The water demon leaped up out of the water and landed just beside Jerry as he walked up. Everyone looked stunned at the scene. Some went for their weapons.

"NOOO!" Fingers yelled and jumped in front of his own brother just in time. The knife that the demon held plunged into his heart. It pulled it back out. The water demon staggered backward, stunned at what Fingers had done. It dropped the knife, puzzled by the human's reaction. Fingers lay on the hard rock as he looked up at the demon.

"I don't take your commands any more," Fingers sputtered out. He fell silent as Jerry held his hands over on the man's chest, hoping to save Fingers from bleeding to death. The rest of the group watched the water demon vanish a second later.

"Jerry, you all right?" Zek asked worried for his friend then noticed his long lost friend lying on the ground. "Fingers," he breathed, horrified that he might loss his brother once again

Fingers looked up to see the halfling and smiled for the first time at seeing his little friend.

"Kill Avlon, for me." Fingers breathed his last words and then faded into darkness. Jerry was beside himself, he cried for the loss of his brother. At least Fingers had saved him from the water demon.

Zek cried for a moment holding onto his old friend, his eye lids narrowed with hatred.

"Kill that thing," Zek ordered the troops.

"That's a water demon, it can't be killed" Jerry said and then saw the determination in the halfling's eye.

The demon sprang out of the water once again, taking up the form of a human. Zek whispered something. It was a magic spell that he had learned a few years ago, and the demon howled in pain as it was made flesh. It realized its life was in danger as the group rushed toward it with swords and axes. It cried at seeing Fingers' body once more before he died. Fingers had given his life for a friend.

"I WANT, AVLON DEAD!" The water demon shouted as the weapons struck him hard into his flesh. He fell to the ground a moment later, feeling the lifeblood flow out of him.

"I take it we're at the border of Trolleon," Bremin asked.

Jerry nodded, shaking off the shock of the demon.

"We're two days away from Hell Mountain, but I haven't seen the other army," Jerry stated. The elves looked concerned about the news.

"You need to double back," a new voice said, and the group turned to look at the stranger. "The elven and human armies are at Small, but they're surrounded, with no way out," Jack informed them.

"Haven't seen you in a couple of months," Zek said. "I thought you and the others had other missions to do."

"I have been busy for that long, but most of the missions are done. I only have two left. When I saw you fall in, I knew you needed to know the situation at Small." Jack stated as he smiled at the small group as he studied them hoping some of them would move.. "What you waiting for, an invitation?" he said with a smirk.

CHAPTER TEN

As dusk fell, Randle and the others looked to their right and noticed the mountain area where the trolls lived. At the base of the mountain range, a few trees could be seen. Anker was looking toward the town off to their left. It had a forest nearby and a small lake. He had fished there once when he was a little younger. He knew it was there, but it was miles away from where the four of them stood.

"So how far is this place?" Dexter asked his father.

Randle looked over at his son while eating an apple. "It's Far," Randle replied, but Dexter wanted to know more than that.

He rephrased the question. "How long will it take us, druid?"

"It's a nine month hike, give or take a few weeks. Though, by the rate we're traveling maybe seven months." Randle threw the apple core away. It landed on the ground several feet away. A small hairy animal walked over to it and sniffed at the core. It liked the smell, it took a small bite, it liked the taste, and then it attacked hungrily.

"You want us to travel eight to nine months to get there?" Dexter exclaimed slightly crest fallen with the idea.

The druid nodded without smiling.

Anker shook his head in disbelief.

"Take it easy, Dexter. We're taking the gate. Randle was only joking." Dexter stated as the other two realized that the druid didn't smile.

"I have other things to worry about," Randle announced. "I have to be back for the fall of Hell Mountain. I'm sure everyone is tied up anyway." He lay on the ground as they set up camp. The druid fell asleep as the others had a meal.

As the sun came up the next day, the group set off for the gate.

"So how far is this gate?" Dale asked, hoping that the druid would tell him and the others.

"It's a three day hike," Randle shouted back since he was ahead of them. *I hate thieves*, he thought. *An unlikely bunch can't trust any of them. Not even the hunter.* He had been dealing with this scum for over a hundred years. He glanced back at the three, but he kept moving forward. Taking a brief look at the far off forest, the druid smiled as they passed through a field that held all kinds of plant life.

By midday, the small group stopped.

"Why aren't we moving?" Dexter asked, annoyed by the small delay.

"We can't go forward," Randle told them.

Anker smiled at the flowers that lay before them. "He's right. Those flowers are deadly."

The other two looked as if they didn't believe the druid or the hunter.

"Flowers aren't deadly," Dale said, unconvinced.

"The last time I warned someone, he didn't listen. Instead, he went in there only to be torn to pieces," Randle informed the two. He had never known his son to forget about the stories from when Dexter was just a child. Once,

Randle had brought him on a trip with a friend.

Dexter now remembered that day, not liking the thought since he had lost a good friend.

"I remember that day. Dez was yelling in pain," Dexter recalled as he tried to forget about the slaughter..

"This way," Randle said as he tried not to smile at his memory. The three followed suit. As the druid led the way, only Dale looked back.

"I'm sure it's not true. I bet an animal attacked that boy," Dale insisted, unsure if he should take their word.

"You don't believe me?" Anker said heatedly. "You're more a fool than that Dez. Those flowers are killers. They've tasted human blood, and they'll tear you apart the moment you step in that field." He grinned hoping that Dale would take the bait. "If you truly want to die, go right ahead. Besides, it'll be better than me killing you once this whole journey is finished. You see, I hunt my prey. Since you stole from me, you'll die either way." Anker started to laugh, enjoying himself way too much. "Go. I dare you!" he said evilly as he toyed with the man.

"If you're so eager to see me dead, I would rather have you hunt me," Dale responded.

The hunter's smile faded, but not for the man that turned down the dare. It was for himself; he really didn't take any pleasure in killing. He would have liked to see someone or something else to do the deed for him.

As the group climbed the small hill, Bremin stuck his head up to see beyond.

"My God," he whispered with surprise and horror in his voice. "Small is surrounded." Then he glanced down at the others to gesture for them to stop. "Don't come any closer," he whispered to the group. He climbed down.

"So, what did you see?" asked Zek. The others nodded in anticipation.

"The others did a good job, but it looks like there's a massive army," Bremin said as he pointed at Talin. "Go to the other side, but be careful about it since Orcs are out there, too."

Talin nodded. He knew how to blend in.

Jerry looked about him as he issued a few commands to his wayward army. All of them were given orders to join certain groups and thin down the ranks of the enemy army that lay in wait.

CHAPTER ELEVEN

"Reid?" Talin called over to the human and then remembered that Reid wasn't there to help them in this situation. "Bob?" Talin said finally.

He looked up to see what the elf wanted of him.

"I need you to find Reid. Tell him it's important," Talin told him.

Bob blinked and bolted like a rabbit.

"He runs as if he's an elf," Talin said, but Bremin knew the truth about the boy. He shrugged off the remark as if it weren't anything.

"The rest of you, we will attack in a few hours, but we need to rest." Bremin said as he went silent. He had to keep an eye out.

Where's Reid? Bob thought as he kept on running until he ran smack into another figure.

"Bob?" Jack said as he got up from the ground, as did the other. "Why are you here?"

"Need Reid's help," Bobby said as he tried to get his breath.

"I'll help you instead, but right now I'm in a bind," Jack said as he pointed north. "A few people from Hamlock are following me. They think I'm Avlon." Then he paused to think about his situation.

"I need Reid's help, not yours," Bobby said determined to figure out what was wrong with this picture.

"Reid is in Small, fool. He's surrounded by armies. Why do you think I went to Hamlock? I have to do his missions for him," Jack stated. He enjoyed toying with people even with his own friends or family.

"You don't understand," Bob said, but Jack was more concerned about his safety and about the approaching group

"I've a bad feeling about this! It might be something that doesn't involve you."

"That's where you're wrong," a stranger said from behind a bush. He looked as if he weren't pleased about something. Four other figures emerged from the bushes.

"I knew Avlon here would get company," one of the men said as he walked up to the two men.

"Besides," Tom winked, trying to tell them that a spy was among them. "I want the two of you in my camp."

"He can't," Bob snarled not pleased with the situation

"His name is Jack, for Sets' sake. Does he look like Avlon? Hell no, If you want something from Avlon, I don't care…" He noticed the bald headed man playing with his sword, which stopped him from speaking.

What did Zek tell me about Fingers? He thought for a moment. As he watched the man flip the sword in the air, his face went white. Jumping into the air higher than any human could, Bob grabbed the hilt of the sword and landed on the ground with both feet as he held out the tip of the blade.

"How dare you!" the balding man said, surprised by the attack.

"No, how dare you, Tekker," Bob breathed with hatred as the group pulled out their weapons. He was surprised at himself. Bob had never moved like that before.

The Tekker moved to counter react, but the tip of the sword inched further into the body.

"You wouldn't kill a fellow human, would you?" the Tekker snarled, but Bob wasn't thinking about the question. All he did was react. Blood ran down the shaft of the sword, and the Tekker felt the tip enter his heart.

"Say hi to O'lin the butcher," Bob threatened the reptilian Tekker and pulled out the sword from its own body, which fell to the ground dead.

"Holy Reich," a dark haired man said and rushed up to his savior. He hugged Bob since he was delighted, which caught him off guard.

"What's going on here?" Jack wanted to know, startled by the reaction.

"Rep here was the one that wanted you dead. I guess you did something to piss Avlon off. Next thing we know, we had orders to find and kill you, but a few things went wrong. I suspected that he was a spy," one of the men said as he pointed to the dead Tekker. "Besides Rep, there are three others running Hamlock. We do fear them, you understand. The town hasn't been the same since they arrived. When Jack here came into the town, I guess you asked way too many questions. That's one of the reasons we came after you. As of the others, dead men don't talk."

Jack and Bob looked a bit startled as the wind blew about them, which caused the trees to sway in the wind.

"What is your name?" Bob asked the man as he smiled

"I'm Tom. This is Dorrin." He pointed at the third of the group. "And that's Ted."

Ted shook their hands, grateful to meet some nice people for a change. "Thanks a bunch," he said with gratitude.

Bob glanced at his brother, who looked back at him. Both were glad the situation was over.

"We've got to go. We have a crisis," Bob stated in a huff since he needed to report to Darren, which piqued Ted's curiosity.

"What sort of problem do you have?" Ted wondered willing to listen to what Bob had to say..

Bob filled them in about the situation and of their plan.

The small group looked at each other and smiled all of them wanted to help in any way they could.

"We'd be glad to help. One small step for the resistance, a giant step for Twilight," Tom said with pride.

CHAPTER TWELVE

Bob and the other four reached the surrounding army the following day. Bremin stood as he studied them.

"More the merrier," Bremin said, glad to see his friends and of the new members that were willing to help in the coming fight. "Talin has found a thousand more on the other side of Small. The ranks are slowly thinning at best, but not fast enough. Can any of you use bows?" he wondered, and the three nodded.

"I learnt to use them. Now I can kill with a single shot," said Dorrin, boasting about his ability, which surprised the elf.

"Don't be so cocky, I just want to hear you say yes," said Bremin as he forced away a smile. He liked their enthusiasm.

The man nodded, not sure if the elf was playing him or not. Walking over to the hill that hid the party, the elf looked over the edge carefully to see the vast army of Orcs and gnomes.

"Jack, where is Reid? He was supposed to be here," Bremin whispered, "but what do you reckon?"

"I reckon we attack at night," Jack suggested, playing off a hunch since he intended to get to Small in any way possible since he had a score to settle with Shannon.

Bremin liked the idea since it was the best way to go about it.

"I need you to sneak past this army to tell the others that we're here," Bremin had ordered the human.

Jack studied the layout of the enemies' camp as he planned his route. "I can--"

"You can, too," Bremin cut him off. "Besides, the others are going to distract their attention while you get in."

"I was going to say I can since it's getting dark." Jack replied in a huff since he was overwhelmed with such feelings. He needed to teach Shannon a lesson, but he could tell it might not happen.

Bremin felt like a fool for interrupting the human.

"I didn't mean...."

"Don't," Jack snapped at the elf. "Besides, Reid is stuck in Small, has been for a few days. That's why I'm here"

"Sorry, I didn't know. How did you find out about the situation?" Bremin wondered impatiently.

Jack didn't want to say since it would betray his master, since it was Brail who had told Jack. Jack just followed the demon's orders to the letter, not willing to question his master at all.

As night settled in around them, Jack trod carefully into the shadows of the massive army. Most of the time he was within the shadows of the little wood that was near the edge of the camp, he just had to make it through the clearing and into the other wood. Jack cast a spell on himself to look like a gnome, a small trick he had learned long ago. One by one, each fire went out as the night wore on. The enemy had no clue that a human was within their camp, he watched them carefully. Making sure that his feet didn't hit any of them.

Now asleep, every beast was slain by the passing figure. It lasted for a long time. Jack was bone-tired. He had no idea how long they had been at it. He heard a bird chirp in the night. *Good,* he thought, *bout time we got through it.* He stepped lightly into the wooded area. After a couple of minutes, a lone figure dropped out of the trees.

"Stop right there," the newcomer warned as he lifted his sword.

"Darren, it's me," Jack said relieved to see him for once in his life.

The man stepped closer to see who was talking to him.

"How did you get though the lines?" Darren asked as he lowered his sword, surprised to see Jack. He had heard that the young man had traveled with Randle some time ago.

"Magic," Jack said the single word. "The rest of us are here beyond this army of monsters." He then stepped lively toward the village.

"Don't," Darren warned. "Sentries may think you're a Tekker. I have to come with you."

As they walked, Jack spied four figures rushing up to them.

"After all the months we've been here, the messenger finally returns," Reid said, as he made his appearance.

"Good to see you, too, Reid. I have some news," Jack said.

"That is?" Reid replied.

"My brother, your friend, Bob is alive and well. He's on the other side of this massive army."

"He's alive?" Reid felt overjoyed at hearing the news. He gave Jack a big hug. Jack stood embarrassed by the hug. Watching the traitor walk into view, he noted the guards surrounded her.

"Can't escape, eh? So, Ricla, what's it like to be a prisoner again?" Jack stated as he walked up to her, he thought about his own betrayal but he ignored it for now. At least no one knew about it just yet.

She didn't reply to the question since it meant nothing to her. She did flinch as he approached. She recognized the human since she was captured at the same time as her; Jack didn't dare say a thing about his own capture. The others did not caution him nor to confront her, since her hands were tied together.

"I take it no one believes you," Jack said to her, at which she laughed evilly.

"None of you will get away with this; Avlon will make sure you don't," Ricla said, but she noticed the confidence in the human's stance. She knew he was going to hit her.

He had no intentions to hit her at all. He just glanced at one of the guards, and he smiled as the guard stuck a pain stick into her side. The pain showed on her face.

"You're going to call off the army, or we'll destroy you," Jack threatened her even more he enjoyed what he was doing.

Again, she laughed as if it were a joke.

"Avlon sent over six thousand troops to seize Small. You will all die," she replied, as she tried to ignore the pain in her side.

Jack shook his head with a slight smile he wanted to teach her a lesson.

"He sent five thousand, no more, no less. Give or take the hundred that died over the night for me to get here," Jack informed her as she studied him up and down.

Her eyes showed surprise for the first time.

"You lie," Ricla snapped, but he leaned closer to her.

His face was only an inch away from hers.

"This resistance has killed half of them. Did they come from the north?" he questioned her. As he tried not to over play his own part, both knew each other, and yet Ricla grinned evilly at him, she too was playing her part in the scheme of things.

"No, you idiot," she answered. "They came from Hell Mountain." She realized that she had been tricked. The group could see her fuming in hatred

"And how many are there in the mountain?" Jack asked.

She was tired of playing mind games with the human. "A skeleton crew of only two thousand is now within the mountain. That's the last of them and there are sentries guarding the mountain." Ricla looked defeated as she told them the truth.

Reid smiled in his own victory as he watched his friend questioning the elf traitor. *Three more missions to go*, he thought, pleased at the outcome. He detected that she was brainwashed by looking at her eyes since he wasn't too far away. As he came toward them, Jack took a step back since he was letting Reid in. Reid touched her forehead with his right hand. She blinked once, then twice, and then she turned her head to see the guards beside her.

"Where's Bremin?" Ricla asked, puzzled about where she was, but the guards ushered her to follow them. Reid stared at her blankly; he had never seen anyone recover that fast before.

She's faking, Reid thought.

A terrifying roar sounded throughout the corridors of the evil base, as gnomes, trolls and Orcs looked up to see what had happened to cause their master to be so angry.

"What's happening in Small?" Avlon demanded as he looked at the gnome.

"Don't know, sir," one of the gnomes replied from its squeaky voice.

His eyes narrowed at the gnome. "You know, don't you?" he shot the question at the troll that stood by the entrance. Avlon advanced on the gnome that quivered with fright.

"We lost contact two weeks ago, sir." The troll responded, feeling dread over come him.

"LOST CONTACT?" Avlon shouted and thought of Randle. *What are you up to, Randle? And why are you undermining my work.* He noticed the two were looking at him. "Gortek, take a small force and find that druid."

Avlon walked over to the only table in the room. He picked up a single glass and drank from it since he had left it there a little while ago.

"What you intend to do, boss?" asked the curious gnome.

The master eyed him, trying to determine why the gnome had asked the question in the first place.

"Why you ask, Ter?" he asked, sneering at the gnome and seeing something that was not there. This gnome was hiding something.

"Just wanted to know, sir," Ter said. He went over to a hole and tried to get some sleep before the new day came. Ter tossed and turned for at least an hour; he just could not get to sleep, the gnome decided to get up out of bed. He walked through the main chamber; he couldn't see Avlon, which was a good sign. He continued to walk to the doors that the trolls guarded. They both opened the door for the gnome without thinking. As he walked down the corridor, several other creatures surrounded him. Several of them

poked at him. Ter didn't care in the least since he knew
they were only playing. He finally emerged into the night
air and away from the rather large group of gnomes.

Freedom, he thought, *is overrated.* He continued to
walk over to the edge, seeing nothing but mountains for
miles on end.

"Ket," Ter called out. "Transport me to Hell
Mountain."

"Did Avlon give you permission?" the other gnome
asked.

Ter nodded. As he saw the portal come to life, he
walked through.

As Randle and his three companions neared the single
gate, he detected something in the far distance, something
evil coming their way. Randle turned and raised his arms to
let them know he needed to say something.

"The land we're going to has no name," he informed
the three. They looked stunned and puzzled at the
statement.

"No name? Are you sure, druid?" Dexter asked feeling
a bit anxious about the trip.

"I am," was the reply. Randle paused for a moment to
gather his thoughts. "When we get there, no one will be
welcoming us."

The three nodded in understanding, but still something
about this trip troubled Dexter.

"Come," his father bellowed, and they walked the last
mile to the gate.

As they walked toward the gate, Randle Arcan Lee
studied the out line of the forest that was a few miles off.
He could see a village at its center. One tower poked out
over the trees, an elven made tower. It looked beautiful in

the sun light. He detected the silver on the outside walls, and yet he was speechless. To the right of the forest lay a field of flowers of all kinds.

Stepping under the arch half an hour later, a tree shaded them from the warm and bright sun for which they were grateful. The druid spoke at last. Each of them was in place waiting for the druid to say the words.

"To the forgotten land," the druid told the arch, and they disappeared, from sight only to reappear in a desert a moment later.

"Not the place," the druid said to the group. "Let's try this again." Gathering himself once more, he noticed a tribe of people running toward them. All of them held spears.

"We better leave, Randle. The natives don't look friendly," Dexter warned.

"In Heaven's name," Arcan tried hoping it would work.

Emerging on the other side, the druid and the other noticed three dragons looking at them, which startled the humans. Dexter tried not to be afraid of them, but he was unsuccessful.

"Can you tell us where the centaurs are?" Randle asked the High Lords as they studied the group with mild interest.

"Not our business," the red dragon said, not willing to tell them, since he wanted the humans to stay. The three dragons had not seen humans in a long time, which unnerved the druid. Randle knew what the dragons would do to them since they licked their lips.

The blue one smiled happily.

"Say glass." it teased.

Once back in position, the druid said the very same words only to find themselves on a very small island.

"You landed us on a rock in the middle of the ocean."

Dexter was annoyed by the outcome. Then he noticed that the water was as clear as a window. "Sea elves," he said, spotting the creatures approach. He pointed at two that were coming toward them. Then he noticed that they were swimming away from something.

"Mermaids," Randle said, intrigued by the show, but he knew the sea elves were swimming away from the mermaids so he formed a fire ball and surrounded it in a bubble. He sent it flying into the ocean, which killed the single mermaid. The two sea elves poked their heads out of the water, glad to see the druid since he had rescued them.

"We thank you druid for saving us. How can we assist you?" both sea elves said at the same time, and then introduced themselves, eager to repay the druid and his friends.

Randle told them where he and his group were trying to go.

"Careful, druid. Centaurs are dangerous. Just say the word centaur. It should take you there. If not, keep trying." One of the sea elves said as the other one flipped some water toward the group, just to be playful. They turned and swam off, grateful that someone had helped them escape.

"You trust them, druid?" Dex asked in wonderment, but the druid didn't seem to hear.

"I'd rather take the word of any elf then a dragon," Randle said, which put a smile on all their faces. The druid and the others went back to the gate, which was only a few steps away.

After a week of going to each and every place on the planet, the druid and the others couldn't think of where else to go.

"Why is it so hard?" the druid said finally. "We've been to more than a dozen places," Randle said angrily and kicked a rock into the woods that wasn't so far away.

"Watch that," a female voice said, stomping out of the near by forest. She brushed her tan pants with her right hand. "That rock hurt me. Now which one of you did that?" she demanded.

Randle's companions pointed at him; he smiled weakly. He noted that she was not pleased to see them. She looked mad, not too much mind you, just enough to deal with the travelers.

"Did you come from the gate?" she said in an angry tone that made Randle's blood ran cold. The druid nodded in agreement.

"We're trying to get to the centaur nation," Randle stated as he backed up from her. "It was I that kicked the rock. I must apologize."

Her face softened somewhat, as she studied the men which all were looking at her. She was beautiful to look at. Her eyes sparkled as her gaze fell upon Dexter; he blushed feeling guilty that he was attracted to her.

"Apology accepted," she said with a smile, now no longer angry with the group or the druid. "I know where it is, but it's hard to get there. It's best to walk it." The female pointed out, eager to help the group since she was trying to find them in the first place.

"We don't have the time to walk it," Randle admitted and paused. "How far is it?"

"It's about a months travel, just south of here," she replied, and then thought of her manners. "Sorry, I'm forgetting my manners. I'm Clare," she said and added, "Since you don't have the time to walk, I'll take you since I'm going that way."

The four watched the woman activate the gate. Touching a single graph, a portal opened.

"Hop in," Clare commanded, but she noticed that they were hesitant. "I won't bite," she teased with a smile.

The four humans walked through the portal, trusting her far too much.

"Come along," Cahler said, who was a leading centaur. He had commanded his own kind for the better part of a century. He was older than the rest of them except for his younger brother "The druid will be here shortly."

Nolt, on the other hand, had ideas for welcoming the druid and his friends. He knew that Cahler had kept the druid from reaching their goal, but now things had changed since he had sent a friend to locate the party of humans.

"Stop that, Nolt," his commander warned. Nolt looked up as he was picking flowers. "Stop that," Cahler repeated. Nolt bowed his head in reply to his brother. He never cared for his brother, but Nolt did listen to him once in a while. This was not one of these times; he had forced his brothers' hand.

The gate powered up and a portal opened. Cahler did a quick study of his men.

"Chin up, brother," Cahler commanded, and turned to see the startled faces of the humans.

"Welcome to Na'ler. I'm Cahler and this is my troop," Cahler said as he bowed for the humans. Nolt snorted, disgusted by his brother's actions

Randle shook his head in puzzlement and looked at his new female friend. "Clare, what's going on?" Randle asked, but she had no idea either. He stared at the centaurs in puzzlement. A small centaur walked up to him.

"It's said in a prophecy that a druid and his friends will come to bring back the centaurs to the known world," Cahler stated. Another snort came from his brother. Cahler ground his teeth, getting upset for no reason. Still, Nolt did not like his brothers' actions or the sucking up.

Randle had an odd smile on his face as did the others. He noticed that the two might have a disagreement of some sort. Randle noticed the bigger centaur holding some flowers.

"Thank you," the druid said, looking pleased as Nolt handed him the flowers. Nolt smiled warmly at him.

"My brother has been trying to stop you from coming for over a week," Nolt said, telling the humans the truth of the matter. "I knew you would come. Clare here is a friend of mine. That's why Clare aided you."

The smaller centaur looked angry with his brother for revealing the truth. Cahler laughed slightly, trying to relieve his own tension.

"My little brother makes up stories. I asked Nolt to pick those flowers," Cahler lied but the small group of centaurs laughed at the thought, undermining their own leader, but they were careful not to upset him even more.

"Nolt speaks the truth. Our commander is a bit of a handful," one of the guards said.

Randle and his friends didn't say a word since they were speechless.

"I'm interested in this prophecy," Randle said to them finally.

"We're to bring you to Duntra," Nolt said, not paying any attention to his brother at the least. "Come, we'll let you ride on our backs," he offered.

Cahler looked even angrier at the suggestion. *No human will ride on my back,* he thought.

"Our ways are different, but we know how to get information. We've sent spies into Avlon's bases and most of them have returned. All but one, a little gnome, though I fear he might have been turned," Nolt stated and then stopped to let the druid speak.

"The main reason to bring your race back is to stop the madness of Avlon Klynn at all cost," Randle said. "He's twisted and evil. We would fall under his spell, but your race is unaffected by Avlon's magic. Who is this gnome you're referring to?"

"His name is Ter. We have no idea what rank Avlon gave him, but he has been gathering information for us," Nolt said calmly, as he started to walk.

Dexter had heard of the name before.

"He's Avlon's main servant. The last I heard, he sent out a troop to recover a lost sword of some kind," Dexter said seeing that the centaurs were looking at him.

Lish, one of the centaurs, smiled at the druid. He wasn't insulted or afraid of the Tekker Avlon. He remembered the war that had happened centuries ago to free the land of Na'ler from the hold of the Tekker Empire. The centaur felt proud that only fifty trekkers were left in the known world. Most of them worked for Avlon now, except a dozen who didn't want any part of the mad Tekker's schemes.

They would help. Besides, it was easier to kill the Tekkers up close.

Seeing two giant trolls fall onto four gnomes, Bremin smiled at himself. "Stupid," he whispered. "They're killing each other now." He began to laugh softly to himself.

"What you up to?" Talin said as he carefully wormed up the hill, so he could not be detected by the enemy, Bremin turned to see one of his own kind walk up to him.

"What's so funny?" Talin asked, and Bremin went head-over-heels as he was laughing so hard. He was enjoying the sight way too much.

"Two trolls... ha-ha... killed...four...gnomes," and he continued to laugh in glee at the thought.

"Not funny," Talin whispered. He looked over the top of the hill to see five hundred troops left to battle it out with each other. The two carefully went back to the others, trying to stay within the shadows of the field.

"I bet they're puzzled that their numbers are decreasing," Reid said, and Bobby looked up to see Reid Lee with his brother Jack Thornstone.

"Brother," they both said not believing their luck to see each other alive and well. They hugged tightly as the others watched the two brothers. Releasing each other, Jack studied Bob to make sure he wasn't a Tekker in disguise. Jack wasn't sure if this was real or not since he wasn't thinking straight lately. He felt as through he was in a dream of some sort. Ever since he had joined Brail and his cause, Jack was being used, but when he encountered his own brother, Bob Thornstone, he kept on testing his own brother to see if he was a Tekker. Meanwhile, Jack no longer cared about the resistance; all he wanted in all of this was money. Pure greed. That was his main reason why Jack joined Brail so long ago. As for Darren and the others, they certainly knew, except for Randle. Darren had a few o f his people keeping at close eye on Jack to see what he would do.

"How did you get out of Small?" Bob finally asked the question that the others were thinking. He realized that he still held an arrow in his hand.

"We snuck out as the enemy killed each other. There are only a thousand left. Once we get rid of most of them, we can surround the last of them," Jack informed them. "We could make ditches and make them into traps."

Bremin liked the suggestion.

"It's best that way. The sooner we can find a way to reverse the spell on them, the better," Zek said, trying to lighten the mood. The group stared at the halfling not knowing what to think of the statement.

"Is it done yet, Zek?" another elf asked hoping that he would know the answer.

"In another hour it will be," Zek called out from beneath the brush and leaves. He was digging up the ground, as several others began to dig as well.

"What are you planning?" Jack asked, since he was curious.

"Wait and see," Bremin said, still smiling about the trolls.

As soon as it turned dark, Jack watched in wonder as the group covered the holes around him. He knew what the plan was; it was to trick the enemy to come their way. He set his feet carefully, trying not to set off any of the traps. Hiding a minute later, a horn sounded in the night just off to his right.

CHAPTER THIRTEEN

After two days of walking for the centaurs, Randle surmised it would have been about a week's worth of human walking.

"Now," Dexter said as he watched the bird's dance, "How did you teach them to dance?"

The gray headed Centaur known as Nolt laughed as he shook his head. "We didn't teach them. The Plinks did, a beautiful six inch tall race," Nolt informed them.

Clare smiled at the thought since she had seen one before.

"They're one of the elven races," Clare piped up which startled the druid.

"Elves in this part of the world?" Dexter asked, glade to know that they were also here. Then he noticed that Cahler was coming over with a slightly bigger version of Nolt. This one had red hair and a battle scar on its neck. "I would like to meet them while we're here," he said to Nolt as the centaur nodded.

"Nolt," said the red heard centaur, with a booming voice that caused the others to look at him. "Please bring the druid over."

Walking up to the main leader, Randle noticed that a book was in the centaur's hands.

"Cahler mentioned that you were interested in the prophecies."

Randle nodded. "I am indeed," he replied as he gazed at the book but not at the centaur. He noticed that the book had an extra flap, which slightly puzzled him. Randle could read the side of the book since it was in clear view. It read, To Our Prophecies and Yours by Trallon Weren.

The great centaur leader handed him the book.

"Study it if you want, but first things first. Do you intend for us to return to Twilight?" the great centaur asked, trying not to tip his hand since they were up to no good.

"Yes, I do intend to bring you back. We need your help to fight off Avlon," Randle answered slowly, but the chief smiled rather warmly at him. Suspicion rolled about in the druids mind. He just could not remember everything about his youth. Randle only recalled certain bits of it. What was he forgetting? That was the main question for him alone.

"I'm Lisha," he told the four. "I govern this tribe. The others are on their way to the gate as we speak. We will be meeting them in two weeks."

Randle looked puzzled by the statement.

"I haven't told you everything…" Randle began only to be cut off.

"Ah, I do know why," said Lisha. "You need us to stop an evil Tekker. And to kill every single thing that falls under his reign of terror"

Still the druid looked surprised by the statement

"How do you know?" Randle remarked. He had not read the full extent of the book to find out their fate. He had only read the first chapter, though Randle Arcan Lee never intended to kill of all of Avlon's forces, which puzzled the druid even more.

"What?" Reid said without thinking and then noticed a troop of Orcs and gnomes come over to see what was going on. They didn't get far before five large Orcs lost their footing and smashed down onto the gnomes that stood just on the edge of the traps.

"Yes!" Bremin cheered. "Twenty gone and more to go." He rushed over, being careful not to be seen in the dark of the night. He looked over his shoulder to see the others, and the mountain that lay northeast of the village. A vast forest separated the two, which pleased him.

"It worked," Jack said with surprise. "It really worked."

Talin stared at him happy as well.

"I take it you thought it wouldn't work?" Talin asked wondering about the human since he was acting weird for the past week.

Jack nodded back with a smile.

"What now, guys?" Jack said too excited to go to sleep.

"Now we rest," Bremin told the group. Then he heard the other traps being set off. "What's going on?" he exclaimed and went over to the small hill and looked over to see the scene before him. Talin armed his bow just in case something happened. "Dear God," he whispered.

He looked over his shoulder to his friends, who saw the horror on his face. Turning his head back, he heard the bowstring as an arrow went flying over his head. He looked up to see a troll overhead as the arrow buried itself in the creature's brain. Bremin rolled to the side quickly as the body slammed on to the ground just was he had been.

"You all right?" Bob asked as he rushed over.

"Sort of…not," he barely said, shaken up from the fright as he then reached down to grab the arrow shaft and pull it out from its mark, wiping it off a second later.

"They know we're here," Bob told him as he pointed at the remains of the army, which advanced on them.

"Fall back," Bremin yelled at the group, and they disappeared into the tall grass, where they had hidden more traps. "This way," he urged, "and stay close."

Following the Bremin in haste, the others could hear screams of pain coming from behind them as Orcs, trolls, and gnomes died in the traps that were waiting for them. One or two escaped for a little while only to be killed by another deadly trap.

Staying hidden from sight, Bremin dared to look back and noticed to his horror that only a hundred foot soldiers were walking away.

"We're safe for the moment," he whispered to the others. *What if their hideout has trolls waiting around the bushes*, he thought. *Dear God, I'd better check.* He took his chance to get a better look and noticed that they were alone after all.

Ushering everyone over, he told them that he didn't think that they were safe. "You three," he said as he pointed to the only humans in the group. "Get back to Small and find out as much as possible. I have a funny feeling that there might be only four to five hundred left. If so, we can trap them," and the group like the idea as they nodded to each other.

"Bremin, what about the holes?" Talin said and the others looked over at him, realizing that he had forgotten about that.

"Fill them in," Bremin commanded and turned away to look over the valley that held the last of their enemy.

"Why cover them when you could use them again?" Jack stated. Reid nodded, as did some of the others.

Turning back, Bremin studied the young man that stood in front of him. "We're not here to kill every one of them. Our mission is to release them from Avlon's power."

Jack wouldn't let it go. "They're better off dead than alive. You can't reverse the spell that Avlon has over them. At least he doesn't control the dead."

Bremin studied the man's face. *Jack's not saying anything and his voice doesn't sound convincing.* "Your logic is prudent, but not sound. I'm the leader here, not you. Now fill in those holes." He commanded as he moved away and heard shovels drop to the ground.

"I'm with Jack," another voice said. "They are better off dead than as Avlon's slaves," Talin admitted, which caught Bremin's attention.

Bremin stopped walking, not liking where this was going. The elf leader had witnessed the extinction of poor animals, man's best friends, and it sickened him. He wasn't happy about it, but he knew that Jack was right. There were thousands of trolls. Killing these would not end the torment, but at least it would free them from Avlon's grip. Walking back to the human, who stood tall, Bremin met the boys' gaze. He didn't like the order he was about to give, since it pained him, but the boys logic was sound.

"You're right. They do need to be freed," Bremin said and looked right into Jack's eyes for the first time. He detected the redness of the boy's eyes but he didn't say a thing. Jack was working for the enemy. Bremin had the feeling for quite some time. This proved his suspicion.

Making their way back to the camp, Bremin looked around him. Something was hiding in the bushes, but he didn't know what it was. It moved a little. Bremin inched carefully over with his sword in hand. His other hand reached out to push away the bush to see the enemy.

"Thank God," Zek said, "I thought I was a goner for sure."

CHAPTER FOURTEEN

Stepping back into the village known as Small, Jack waved over his companions.

"Who's this?" Reid asked, and he looked surprised to see the dwarf with him. "Gandis, what are you doing here?" The dwarf laughed heartily at the thought.

"I'm Jandis. Gandis is my twin brother. Don't you remember?" the dwarf replied in good spirits.

Reid blushed at the thought since he had forgotten about the twin since he hadn't seen him in quite some time, Reid realizing now that he had made an error.

"I'm so sorry, I wasn't thinking" he told the dwarf feeling foolish about the mistake.

"No need. It happens all the time. Besides, it's kind of handy at times. I had to fill in holes for him once when we were slaves." He laughed at the thought. "One time, he was whipped for sitting down. When the guard left, I made my brother go to sleep as I continued his work for him." Then he slammed his hand on to the rock, showing them what he had to do. "See that broken rock?" he said. The others looked at it as Jandis picked the rock up with his bare hands. He tightened his grip as the rock crumbled through his fingers. His friends were amazed that the dwarf could break the huge rock with his own hands.

"You broke that," Jack wondered, still amazed at the sight, "with your hands?"

The dwarf nodded. "Aye. I can do more than that. I once killed an Orc with my bare hands."

The group began to laugh, not believing a single word, but Jandis was telling them the truth. He didn't care if they believed him or not. He told them his tale of what had happened for just the entertainment of telling a story.

"Let's go," Jandis said, "to the bar to get something to eat." He patted his stomach and everyone else saw him go to the inn, but the thing was Jandis was always hungry. Whether it was raining or not, or when he was on a long hike. He always thought about food.

Jack watched Jandis walk away, he had things to do, but he had to keep up his bargain for Avlon and for Brail. He had sworn an oath to both of them, so he could gather information for either of them. He didn't feel guilty for his own betrayal; he just didn't care about the outcome of the war. One way or another, all Jack wanted to be left alone.

Jack knew he had to report to Darren.

"I'll catch up soon," he said to Bremin and rushed off to see their human leader.

Standing in plain view, Darren looked at the beautiful sight but knew that danger lurked around the corner. Turning away a moment later, a lone figure came up from behind him.

"Darren," Jack said as he walked over to him. "Any news of surviving trolls?"

"Just two. I saw them get up a few minutes ago, but I fear your traps may not work this time," Darren informed him. Jack just smiled at the thought as he contemplated telling a lie to cover his own tracks. Darren caught the look for a moment. Both dismissed it for the moment, but Darren would keep it for future reference, and Darren asked another question. "Did the other side suffer?"

The man in front of him gave him a slight grin. "They did. Most of them have died, but the rest are missing." Jack had the urge to tell him where they went but thought better of it. "Bremin's traps got them. You should have seen it. They rushed us as if they were wolves. We thought we were dead, but most of them died in the traps that we laid for them. I would say about two hundred of them died last night."

Open-mouthed in shock at the good news, Darren noticed his wife walking up to them.

"Hon," he said excitedly, as she walked with her guards, since she was returning from her little trip. "Seems like we're winning," Darren said then he saw an arrow fly towards her.

"Duck!" he yelled in warning. His wife twisted around, grabbed the arrow before it reached its mark, and then looked over at the person that shot it. Darren had never seen his wife do that before, but he knew that she was a warrior nonetheless. She had trained with the best that he could afford. The way she moved was told him that she was confident in her abilities.

"You," she said coldly and evenly, as her eyes drifted over to the traitor. "Seize her." Willow called out commanding two of her troops to seize the elf. Backing away, Ricla the elf Princess was seized from behind by two of her own people.

"Come along, traitor," one of them said in a manner that could freeze your blood. All the men kept staring at her as she walked; they knew she had betrayed them long ago, but faking her death was another thing. Her head held high, she whispered something that caught Darren's attention.

"What did you say, bitch?" Darren demanded, slapped her across the face, and then walked over to his wife.

"You'll be slaughtered at Hell Mountain," said Ricla, but Jack laughed at the thought. "Why are you laughing?" Ricla demanded furiously.

"Where do you think that army came from?" Jack said, not thinking about himself for a moment. "They came from Hell Mountain," and she tried to break free from the guards.

"You lie!" she screamed in fury. "Avlon will punish you for what you've done, traitor."

Darren looked from Jack to Ricla. He had heard that news before, but he couldn't fathom why she called him a traitor.

"He's telling the truth," Darren stated and scratched his chin. He had the feeling that Jack was a traitor, and this proved it. *I bet Avlon sent him in as a spy.*

Ricla started to grin as she noticed movement in the bushes behind the two men.

"Look..." she warned, but it was too late. An axe tore into Jack's left side. He yelled out in pain as it wounded him greatly. Darren fell to the ground and moved to his right as an Orc slammed an axe into the ground next to him.

"Attack!" Ricla shouted, but the two elves wouldn't let go. They saw to their horror that the last of the army was waiting to attack them.

"You hear that?" Jandis said with a full mouth. He looked out the window of the inn and saw the scene. He swallowed at what he saw. "It's a surprise attack!" he yelled to the rest of the group and picked up his battle-axe. All of the warriors in the inn started to spill out the doors, each holding their weapons as Orcs ran toward them swinging their weapons.

Rushing outside, Shannon Lee grabbed two of the swords that hung from his belt and ran into the attacking army, cutting into them. He hoped that Avlon's army would not recognize him. A single Orc looked his way, surprised to see him.

"General," one of the Orc's said in surprise. Shannon's hand had been exposed. He had to get rid of the advancing army. Every single one died on impact. Reaching the centre, he dropped the two swords that he was carrying and reached into his hidden pocket to reveal his secret. Grabbing the sea sword by the hilt, he pulled out the blade and held it high for all to see. Both armies stopped, stunned by seeing a single knife that glistened in the light. Orcs cried out a warning, but they just could not move. The knife expanded into a sword, which made them go stiff. Trolls stared at the young man as dread came to their faces. They knew who he was. It was the boy who had returned from his home country, he was feared and at the same time these Orcs and trolls took his commands no matter what.

Shannon whispered something. A bright light surrounded the group and the enemy, and then it went out just as quickly, leaving only the good people untouched.

Darren stood not believing his luck. Every troll and gnome was gone from sight.

As Jack made a slight sound, he cursed under his breath the others crowded around looking down.

"He's not dead," Darren said and pulled the axe out of him carefully.

"What the…" Ricla managed to get out since she was stunned as of everyone else.

Shannon went over to the wounded man and bent

down. His hands hovered over the wound.

"You'll be fine in a minute," he assured Jack, recognizing him now. He had seen him before this whole adventure had begun. Talin and the others walked over to see that Jack was much better already. Helping him up, Shannon smiled faintly at them.

"Who are you?" Darren said and the young man looked him in the eye.

"What do you think?" he murmured.

"You're Randle's nephew," Darren sputtered, not believing his luck. He had heard of the young man and of the many tales that he had heard over the years.

Bob rushed to his brother's side, seeing that he hadn't lost him after all.

"Thank you," he said, grateful for the miracle.

Shannon studied the group. He chose his words carefully. He felt disgusted at what he had done.

"Don't thank me. I'm the one that betrayed you." Shannon stated. He knew it was a lie, but he just couldn't let Jack take the fall. Then he turned away and began to walk away.

"You did this?" Darren shouted in fury. "Why?"

This caused Shannon to turn around. He first looked at Jack, and then shifted his eyes to Darren. "I only wanted to collect my gold and be done with all of you." Then he continued to walk off.

Two elves came down from the trees. While staying close to his wife, Darren looked over at them, smiling at his beautiful wife. He could feel the pain in his shoulder, since he had been hit by an arrow, but he ignored it for now.

As Jandis got to his feet, he noticed his brother.

"Gandis," he breathed, and both grinned at each other. "We noticed something was wrong, so we came over to help." The two hugged for a quick moment.

"It's good to see you, Jandis. It's been far too long, but I've written songs of my journey with these fine people."

"What?" Ricla said, still being held. "Twins?" she whispered, and then looked away disgusted at the sight.

"You should die, Princess," the two growled, but Willow stepped over to them.

"She's worth more alive than dead. She holds more secrets about Avlon than any of us will ever know or wish to know," Willow said and stared at the Princess coldly.

Both dwarves chuckled.

"Ask Shannon. He knows a lot more than he's letting on." This caught Darren's attention. "He's protecting someone here. I don't know who, but he took the blame for this mess."

"Listen and listen well, Ricla," Willow said. "You'll tell us everything that we want to know and more."

The traitor spat at Willow's feet.

"I'll never tell." Ricla shook her head, but it didn't stop Willow from walking over to her husband. She glared back at the elven traitor.

"You'll talk one way or another." Willow looked into Darren's eyes. He looked back into her eyes. All he wanted to do at this moment was to kiss his wife, and he had missed her. He bent forward and she to him. A happy tear fell from his face onto her as they kissed.

"Anyone dead?" Reid called out and saw the two armies side by side.

"All accounted for," a big man said and looked at the elves, still sweating up a storm. Jerry looked at his friend and shook his head; he could tell that Doyle had lost some weight but not much.

"Same here," an elf said, "but I fear many of us are

wounded." He removed his hand from his shoulder, from which the blood oozed out.

"We can help," a villager called out. "We have more supplies than we need."

Every villager helped to tend to the wounded throughout the morning.

"Easy there," a beautiful lady said to Darren as she slid the arrow shaft out from his upper arm.

"That hurt you know," he said with gritted teeth.

She smiled. "It would hurt more if I didn't take off the end first." Then she looked at the wound with the arrowhead still in it.

"What's your name?" he asked seeing her silver eyes for the first time. She took his breath away, and he looked stunned. Glancing at the other villagers, he now knew why the enemy had come to this village. These people were not human. They were dragons in human form. That's why Avlon sent his army; these people were a threat to him.

"Alice," she told him as she put on the medication.

"Ahhh!" he yelled and settled down once the pain went away.

"You can't handle pain," she told him.

"You're not--" he began only to be interrupted by her piercing eyes.

"We're dragons," she whispered. "We gave up the fight long ago."

Darren felt the last of the pain wash over him. "We can handle pain just fine. It's just that people like you make it worse," he complained, covering up her whispering.

"Have you ever given birth?" she replied, seeing what he was trying to do.

"Could you help now?" he whispered back, and she shook her head at the question.

"No, we will not." Alice replied. "You didn't answer my question," she said aloud. "The dragon nation does not help humans," she whispered harshly.

Darren looked up to see his wife walking over.

"I believe you, and no to your question, I have never given birth, but I can understand pain and sadness, I lost my family long ago." Darren informed Alice as he noticed his wife standing next to him. He remembered the day when Skull, a friend of his, had told him that his parents had died in a fire. Darren found out later in life that it was true; Avlon had ordered his men to kill off his parents. Sadness filled his soul, he forced back the tears, but one slipped out.

"He's impossible," Willow said and smiled as she noticed that his arm was wrapped in a bandage. She noticed the tear for the first time. Willow had never known her husband's true ambition or his great secret.

"Will he be okay?" Bob asked the man tending to Tunalun's wounds. Bob had begun to befriend the elf prince.

"He got more arrows in him any anyone else. It's a miracle that he's still alive."

Bob looked up to see Reid walk over as the doctor poured healing water over the wounds. Behind Reid, Jack followed and saw the magic of the water take effect on the elf.

Darren called everyone over since he had something to say. All of them surrounded him, wanting to hear what the next move was.

"Once we get rid of their dead and heal our wounded, we can move on to Hell Mountain. When we get there, we have to make sure that an army is not out side. If there are sentries, I would rather have the elves take them out," he announced, and they all cheered waiting eagerly to cause more problems for Avlon.

CHAPTER FIFTEEN

Nearing troll Rock, Randle and the others of his group noticed Cahler was limping a bit since he had stubbed his foot against a tree root that they had passed a few minutes ago. Dexter only shook his head.

"You all right?" Randle asked, concerned for his newfound friend.

"I just kicked a root is all," the centaur informed him, but Arcan had his mind elsewhere.

I sure hope Reid's okay. I hope he gets the witch to help us. Then he smiled when he remembered when Reid found out that Randle was his father. Pleasant memories for both of them. Randle took a single step only to meet another foot under his.

"A bit distracted?" Dexter asked the druid as he moved his foot out of the way.

Looking over his shoulder at the centaurs, Randle was still puzzled over the meeting that they had. "Where did the other troop go?" Arcan asked the commander.

"To make villages throughout the land, so that way we can make a difference," the commander told him, but Dexter had a bad feeling about them. What it was he didn't know. When they were in Na'ler, the druid had to tell them where to go. Why did the centaurs really leave? He thought, and why did they let Randle summon the gate for them? All good questions for the druid, but Dexter, on the other hand, didn't want to look foolish.

"Can you tell me why you left?" the druid asked the centaur.

Looking nervous, Cahler was startled by the question. "W-we...left because it seemed to be the right thing at the time," the centaur lied.

Glancing at Dexter, the druid nodded, understanding the need to know the basics, but the centaurs had other plans for them, plans he didn't know about.

"I sure hope you don't try to betray our trust," the druid said coldly.

"Wouldn't dream of it, druid. Besides, before Avlon there was Mark the Terrible. We opposed him since he tortured our kind. We banded together and fought him for a long time. In the end, we won and conquered the known land," but the leader didn't realize that he gave out too much information.

Dust clouds formed before him something was making their way to them.

"What do we have here?" Nolt said then ran toward them. "Beastly men," he puffed as he returned, catching his breath from the run. "As tall as two men, but grey all over," he sputtered out.

"Ogres," Randle said. "They must have spotted us from the mountains."

Setting up his troop a minute later, Cahler noticed the small group of humans guarding their rear. Over a hundred Ogres surrounded them, attacking all sides. Centaurs were killing them; their blades smashing into living flesh, killing the beastly men that Avlon's spell had control over. Bodies littered the ground. All of the centaurs were killing them.

All of them had blood rage. Cahler tore into them as if they were paper, rearing up on his hind legs.

Randle could see their eyes ablaze.

"He's in frenzy," he told his small group. He realized why they had left Twilight so long ago. "Oh, no," the druid muttered as he now realized why the Centaurs had been banished. "I brought killers back," he whispered.

"Something wrong, druid?" Nolt asked as he walked up to him.

"Nothing," the druid replied. "I just remembered that I have to report back at the keep." He leaned in to whisper to his small group. "I'll be back. Dexter, you're in charge." Then he disappeared a second later as Cahler looked at Dexter with a menacing smile.

"Run," he ordered his men and they ran like the wind. None of the centaurs gave chase.

Nolt smiled evilly at his commander.

"Twilight will burn," he said passionately.

Cahler smiled. "Avlon must be keeping Mark the Terrible somewhere. We will find you, master."

Appearing in the old druid castle, one of the elders looked up to see Randle.

"Haven't seen you in months," the white bearded druid said, as he shook the younger man's hand. Randle smiled faintly.

"It's good to see you too, Bore. I think I may have done something stupid. I need the book of centaurs," Randle said in a rush.

The old druid handed him the book. "How so?" Bore asked.

"I just released the Centaurs from exile," Randle informed him.

Bore's face went deathly white with fear.

"You've been tricked. They will locate their former master and, in doing so, they will murder us all," Bore informed his young friend.

"Who is their master?" Randle asked.

"He's worse than Avlon. If he replaces Avlon, all will fall. He's Mark the Terrible."

A cold shiver went down Randle's spine; he had been tricked in deed. His mouth hung open in shook.

"Prepare for war," Randle said. "We must put a stop to this."

Bore just shook his head; he looked gravely horrified at the news. His nightmare from the night before was coming true, but Bore knew that all of them had to fight a terrible war. He feared for the people of twilight of what the centaurs might do to them.

"I'll prepare the others for open war."

CHAPTER SIXTEEN

Ten elves stayed within the shadow of the mountain. All of them had marked their targets. Since he had recovered, Tunalun was one of the elves that were picked for this mission. An Orc passed by him, its back to him. Tun looked over his shoulder to see if the area was clear and it was. Staying behind the Orc, he treaded carefully so he could not be heard. He drew out his sword, coming near enough but not too near to be detected. Tunalun swung his sword and sliced the Orc's head off.

Each of the other sentries were taken care of, while Tunalun stood overseeing the far off village that they had helped. This area had a few trees, at the base of the mountain lay a small lake with a few bushes and shrubs.

The rest waited outside of Hell Mountain, the human, elven, and dwarven army had hidden themselves behind several rocks, but only two scouts went in to take a look, followed by a small band of the fighters.

This is a bad idea, Talin, Zek thought as he clutched the bag, which contained the elf stones. He peered into the darkness of the cave to see what was going on. They had his back all right, but for how long? That he wanted to know.

Randle appeared in front of him. Before he could speak, the druid shook his head, warning him not to. *The druid looks concerned about something,* Zek thought. Inch by inch, they traveled, seeing slaves hard at work. Twelve men followed the scouts who got rid of the guards so they could free the slaves. A dwarf slave and several others pointed toward the next tunnel, telling them where to go. They all went unnoticed for most of the morning freeing all sorts of races, humans, dwarves, and elves. By mid-day, the group reached the core of the mountain. Peering in, Zek spotted a lone gnome, the first and only one he saw in here. Zek thought about the other groups that were freeing others hidden within the mountain.

"Ter," shouted a Tekker. "Where's my back up army?" he said coldly to the gnome, but Ter had planned on this. He knew Avlon and his great army was going to fail. He had worked with his enemy for so long. He and the others of his kind weren't affected by Avlon's magic at all.

"They should be here soon," Ter lied and backed off. "Besides, Limp. You should take Avlon's place," the gnome said to the Tekker, and he smiled at the thought.

"Nice try, Ter. But that's a pipe dream." Limp looked away since he heard fighting in the corridors. "How's that possible? A surprise attack? Who would do this to me," Limp cried out, not one of his men came to help him or the gnome.

Lent appeared at the door and smiled happily.

"Well, well. I see a Tekker," Lent said as he took a step further. He never saw the gnome since Ter had hidden himself behind a rather large rock.

"We--" Limp began and then realized that the new army was there, just waiting for the command. Elves, men, and dwarves poured out into the vast chamber as they fought with all their might as hordes of trolls rushed out from every direction. Zek was caught in the middle of the room as well of the druid. Lightning lanced out of the druids fingers, killing troll after troll, but more came in. He alone heard laughter, and he glanced over his shoulder to see Lent lying dead or near death as he was on the ground. Over him stood a Tekker. Randle grew mad and his lightning bolts changed colors to a deathly red.

With his other hand, he pointed to a bunch of trolls that surrounded the halfling, and a thin, red lightning bolt embedded itself in the ground, which caused the trolls to disappear. Randle reached down to get the elf stones only to remember that Zek had them. Everywhere he looked, he couldn't see the halfling.

"Zek!" Randle shouted as Orcs swarmed about him. Concerned that the halfling was in trouble, he turned slightly and noticed that the halfling was battling six large trolls.

"Stay away," Zek warned the surrounding trolls, "or I'll use these stones," but they paid no attention to what he was saying. He twisted away just as four hands reached for him. He jumped away only to land near the end of the ledge. "I said stay away," he warned, but a troll touched the pouch and it burned his hand.

Thinking fast, Zek grabbed the pouch and brought the green elf stones out.

"ZEK, NO!" Randle yelled in warning as fear enveloped him. He couldn't allow Zek to die by the hands of trolls, but the halfling couldn't hear him at all.

The trolls stopped in their attack and saw the beauty of the elf stones. Zek reached up with his right hand that held the stones, and a great green light began to glow in the darkness. It became one with Zek, reaching out to encompass whoever was nearby. The green glow went on forever. No one battled; they all stood where they were.

By now, all of Hell Mountain looked green. For Randle and the resistance, whoever was wounded was healed; the dead soldiers came back to life and rose to their feet. The light disappeared as quickly as it came, taking Avlon's army with it.

Limp looked defeated as he noticed that he was alone, his great army lost. The Tekker wasn't touched or taken away for some reason.

"Hi, Limp. Remember me," Randle said coldly with narrowed eyes as he strolled over to the Tekker. The Tekker looked puzzled, staring into the druid's eyes and not knowing who the old man was.

"It's me, Randle," the druid told the Tekker, who went deathly white as he realized that Avlon's old apprentice stood before him.

"No," Limp said, not believing it was truly him.

Randle lifted one of his arms.

"Now die," Randle Arcan Lee whispered as a blue lightening bolt raked through the Tekker's body, hurting him in every way possible. He fell dead at Arcan's feet a minute later.

"What?" Bremin asked as he rushed over to Lent, not believing that the green light had brought back the dead. "For a minute there, I thought you were dead," Bremin said to his friend.

"I thought I was, too," Lent admitted as he dusted himself off.

Back outside in the fresh air, the rather large army tended to it's wounded, but couldn't help the dead that had fought outside of the mountain. Twenty good men died that day, fighting for a better future. The elf stones had not reached as far as those on the outside of the mountain.

Darren and the others watched the druid and his small group as they prepared to journey on. Darren was puzzled by this. The druid walked up to him.

"Darren, I need you to do something," Randle said as the man stared into the druid's eyes.

"What is it?" Darren asked since he wanted to hear what the druid had to say..

"There's a man called Shelp in Blume. He runs an inn in the middle of town. You can't miss him. I need him in our cause."

Darren nodded, understanding how much the druid was willing to do for their freedom.

"I've never been there," Darren admitted as he smiled. "It's said they have beer. I've never had it."

Randle nodded he had been there once since he had family there.

"You'll like it. Anyway, I have a few things to settle up." He moved away from sight.

"Randle," the halfling called, drawing the druid's attention. "You see what I did?" Zek said excitedly.

The druid smiled as he gazed at the halfling who smiled back.

"We all did. I heard about your loss," Randle replied, and the halfling looked down at the ground remembering his friend's death.

"Zek, I need you for a mission of great importance," Randle said, and the halfling's eyes lit up, happy at the thought. "There is a lost jewel just east of the town of Ternel," the druid informed him.

The little man nodded with great care. "I'll leave right

away," Zek announced.

"Hold on, Zek," Randle said. "Take your time, and take backup just in case something bad happens."

Then he noticed Bremin was waving him over.

"Randle, I feel different," Zek said as the druid looked back at him, with concern in his eyes. He had grown to like the halfling in his own way.

"What sort of different? Can you describe it?" Randle wondered.

"I feel good, different. As if the weight of the world had been lifted from my shoulders," Zek responded, not sure if he should be feeling this way.

Bremin had heard the conversation. "Randle, you okay?" Bremin asked as the druid took a few steps toward him. Zek stayed where he was to hear all this.

"No, I've done something terrible," Randle replied.

"What is it?" Bremin asked, since he was concerned for his friend.

"I found the centaurs," he admitted.

"Why's that so bad?" Bremin asked, wondering what else to say.

"They are worse than I thought."

Bremin shook his head, not believing in their bad luck.

"Our next step is to free the people in the east. It'll take over a year to get there, but there are other holds along the way. Smaller, I grant you, just focus on them first, after you get Shelp of course," the druid instructed.

"What if we encounter a hold on our way to Blume?" Bremin asked.

"Free it," Randle stated as he smiled at the thought.

Moving away from the others, Randle needed his rest for a short time. He knew he had only a month to rest. *It'll help*, he thought and walked out into the meadow. He looked back for a moment. At first, he saw a figure looking at him from the forest. He blinked and noticed it was gone. *So you're back, Shannon,* he thought. *At least we defeated Hell Mountain.* He smiled since he was happy; it was the first time in eight years that the two had seen each other, back when Randle had killed an important Orc, Nesk, one of Avlon's trusted lieutenants.

As the master of East Side Edge sat in his chair, overlooking everything, a gnome came into his chamber.

"Who dares bothers me?" a female Tekker said coldly and set her eyes on the yellow creature.

"Ter," the gnome said and swallowed. "Hell Mountain has been defeated by Randle, my lord."

She smiled evilly as she rose from the stone cold chair, towering over the gnome.

"I already know that rodent." Sabena beckoned two of her guards over. "Your reign of deceit has finished," she said menacingly and smiled at the small gnome, who laughed as if he had enjoyed a joke.

"The centaurs have come back from their prison. They will serve me and me alone," Sabena said as her eyes sparkled with hatred. "Take him away," she commanded her guards. As she looked their way, Sabena saw two large centaurs enter her chamber. Both Orcs turned to attack them, only to be slaughtered on the spot.

Ter smiled at the centaur.

"Hi, Nolt," Ter said. "Long time, no see.."

Nolt smiled at the stunned Tekker as he swung his mighty axe with all his might, slicing her head clean off her body.